the CHRISTMAS BUS

the CHRISTMAS BUS

Melody Carlson

**Doubleday Large Print
Home Library Edition**

Revell
Grand Rapids, Michigan

Published by Fleming H. Revell
a division of Baker Publishing Group
P.O. Box 6287, Grand Rapids, MI 49516-6287
www.revellbooks.com

Printed in the United States of America

ISBN 13: 978-0-7394-7487-7

Scripture is taken from *The Message* by Eugene H. Peterson, copyright © 1993, 1994, 1995, 2000, 2001, 2002. Used by permission of NavPress Publishing Group. All rights reserved.

**This Large Print Book carries the
Seal of Approval of N.A.V.H.**

Stay on good terms with each other, held together by love. Be ready with a meal or a bed when it's needed. Why, some have extended hospitality to angels without ever knowing it!

Hebrews 13:1–2

Prologue

December 20

"Where in the world are we?" asked Amy as she pulled the wool blanket she was using as a shawl a little tighter around her shoulders. She looked out the dirt-streaked passenger window, gazing at the bleak, brown rolling hills all around them.

"Like I told you . . ." Collin pulled into the slow-moving vehicle lane to allow a short string of cars to pass him. "We're in northern Oregon now. We'll be heading into the Cascade Mountains in a few minutes. I just hope we can make it over without too much trouble. Ol' Queenie almost bought the farm going over the Rockies."

At the beginning of their cross-country trip, they had christened their revamped school bus the "Queen Mary" but had since shortened it to "Queenie." The name worked since the makeshift motor home was as big as a ship and probably used about as much fuel too. Collin hadn't told Amy that they were almost out of money, due to the recently inflated gas prices, or that he was worried about Queenie's transmission going out before they reached their final destination in San Diego.

"I just hope I can make it over without *another* rest stop." Amy rubbed her hand over her large taut belly, silently promising her unborn baby that everything was going to be okay, that they would be settled in sunny Southern California in time for Christmas, which was only five days away.

"So why did we come this way?" she asked as they started the ascent into the foothills. More vegetation was growing here. Mostly evergreens, but the change of scenery was welcome after so many miles of barren, dry land.

Collin shrugged. "I don't know. It just looked like a straight shot on the map to me."

"It seems pretty desolate up here."

"There'll be more towns once we get over this pass," Collin assured her. Then he pointed to a sign. "See, it says, 'Christmas Valley, eleven miles.'"

"Oh, I got a free pamphlet about that town at the last gas station," she said suddenly, reaching for her oversized bag. She foraged until she found the dog-eared brochure. "Here it is." And then she began to read. "'Tucked into a protected niche of the eastern Cascades lies the sleepy little town of Christmas Valley. This quaint little hamlet received its name two centuries ago when a pair of stranded fur trappers sought refuge during the Christmas blizzard of 1847.'" She stopped reading and looked out the window again, shuddering as she peered up at the heavy-looking gray clouds overhead. "Do you think it's going to snow, Collin?"

"Hope not." He kept his focus on the road, and she turned her attention back to the brochure.

"'Since that frosty winter,'" she read, "'the town has gone from a spot on the map to an unimpressive trading post, to a rather insignificant mining settlement, to a thriving logging community with a working railroad.

Then the recession of the eighties arrived, and the logging industry diminished due to environmental concerns that listed the spotted owl as endangered and, not long after that, the boreal toad as well.'"

Collin laughed. "What is a boreal toad?"

She shook her head. "I don't know, but it sounds like it was trouble for Christmas Valley."

"So then what happened?"

"It says that the railroad was rerouted and that Christmas Valley was forced to reinvent itself or disappear." She skimmed the words, worried that she might be getting carsick again. "It basically sounds like the town decided to capitalize on its name—Christmas Valley—and it turned into a tourist town where everything is all about Christmas."

"Interesting . . ."

Amy looked out at the pine trees. It was getting dusky now. "I guess it does look kind of Christmassy up here. But it would be better with snow." And even as she said this, almost like magic, fluffy snowflakes started to fall, spinning from the sky, hitting the windshield in big white splotches. "Look, Collin!" she cried out with childlike happiness. "It *is* snowing! It's really snowing."

But Collin just groaned as he turned on the wipers. Snow was the last thing he needed right now.

"It's going to be a white Christmas for someone!" she exclaimed.

Collin just muttered, "Uh-huh," and tried to shift into a lower gear. He didn't know a lot about engines or mechanical things, but he knew that the grinding sounds coming out of Queenie seemed to be getting worse and worse. He also knew that they were probably not going to make it over the mountain pass tonight.

"Maybe we should check out this town," he said as another sign appeared, this one announcing that the exit to Christmas Valley was only a mile away.

"Could we?" she exclaimed.

"Why not."

And so it was that a rather large and brightly painted bus rolled into the quiet little hamlet of Christmas Valley.

"'Population of 2,142,'" announced Amy as she read the welcome sign on the edge of town. It was after five o'clock now, and it appeared that most of the businesses, which weren't many, primarily a grocery store, hardware store, and barbershop, as well as about a dozen or so small retail shops that seemed to be specifically related to Christmas, were already closed.

"Oh, look," said Amy, "there's the North Pole Coffee Shop." She laughed and pointed across the street. "And there's Mrs. Santa's Diner. This is so cute!"

Collin parked on the main street, right in front of the diner, and they both got out and looked up and down the mostly deserted street. The snow was falling harder now, but Amy seemed happier than she'd been for the entire trip as she pointed out all the various Christmas decorations and shops. It was as if she were her old happy self again, and Collin decided to make the best of it.

"Let's get something to eat," he told her. They went into Mrs. Santa's Diner, sat down, and ordered Blitzen burgers (all the main food items were named after Santa's eight reindeer).

"You folks just passing through?" asked a woman wearing a Santa cap and a red-and-white-striped apron with "Mrs. Santa" embroidered across the front, although Collin had heard someone else calling her "Gloria."

"Yeah," said Collin as he dug out enough cash to pay the bill, along with a very meager tip. "But I think we'll probably spend the night in town."

"That your bus out there?" asked a voice from behind him. Collin turned to see a uniformed policeman. He seemed to be studying the couple with an expression that appeared not too welcoming, not to mention un-Christmassy.

"Yes," Collin nodded politely. He didn't want trouble.

"Well, you'll have to move it."

"But I didn't see any 'No Parking' signs."

"That may be so, but you can't leave it out there on the street. We have ordinances against camping in town. And didn't I hear you say you were planning to spend the night?"

Collin glanced over at Amy, who looked hopeful. "Yes, my wife is pregnant, and this long trip has been hard on her. I thought we might spend a night here." Of course, he didn't want to mention his possible mechanical problems being a concern as well. He didn't want to upset Amy.

"Well, there's a nice bed and breakfast," said Gloria as she wiped down the countertop. "It's called the Shepherd's Inn and is within walking distance from town. It's small, but nice. They only have about five or six rooms, but last I heard they weren't all rented out yet."

"Thank you," said Collin. He listened as she gave specific directions.

"That sounds easy enough," said Amy, smiling up at the policeman. He nodded, as if this plan met with his approval, and then wished them a somewhat restrained "Merry Christmas."

The snow was coming down even harder as Collin and Amy went back out onto the street. "It's going to be cold tonight," said Amy as they hurried to the bus.

"We'll be okay," said Collin with false confidence, but he quickly shut the door to keep the chill out. He forced a smile as he climbed into the driver's seat. "Well, let's go find this little inn."

But instead of going directly to the inn, Collin took them on a full tour of the little town. Of course, there wasn't much to see, but he stretched it out as long as he could, going by the post office and the grade school and through the surrounding neighborhoods until he was going down Main Street again.

"It seems like you're stalling," Amy finally

said in tired exasperation. "Why don't we just go to the inn now?"

"Yeah . . ." he said slowly. "The thing is, Amy, we don't really have enough money to stay there, at the inn I mean. It would probably take the rest of our gas money for just one night."

Amy laughed. "I didn't think we were actually going to stay in the bed and breakfast, Collin. As nice as that sounds, I figured we were just going to park there to keep the policeman happy."

Collin chuckled as he turned the big bus up the street that led to the Shepherd's Inn. "Hey, then you figured right."

1

December 14

It'd been nearly twenty-five years since Christmas Valley's discouraged business owners had first gathered to determine the fate of their faltering economy. That's when they decided it was high time to capitalize on the town's seasonal name.

"Christmas Valley to become the Christmas capital of the Pacific Northwest," the headlines in their little weekly paper had read back in 1980, and that's when the CVA (Christmas Valley Association) had been established. It started out simply enough, things like raising funds to purchase Christmas lights and basic decorations as well as scheduling some civic activities during the month of December, but over the years it had evolved into something of a Christmastime three-ring circus, which now launched itself shortly after Halloween.

"Gotta make the most of the season," Mayor Drummel (aka Santa Claus) would tell the CVA at their annual planning session in late March. And make the most of it they did. But by early December, some of the townsfolk, weary of this never-ending holi-day, could be overheard murmuring things like, "I'm sick of Christmas," or "One more chorus of Jingle Bells and I'll . . ." And some less festive folks had adopted the snowbird way of life, flocking down to Phoenix or Palm Springs at the first sight of a candy cane.

But that was never the case with Edith Ryan, the optimistic owner and operator of the Shepherd's Inn. Edith always looked for-ward to this time of year with unbridled en-thusiasm. "I wouldn't mind if Christmas lasted forever," she'd been known to tell friends and neighbors as she happily pre-pared for the holiday, cooking and decorat-ing for her family (which now consisted of four grown children and their various spouses plus five grandchildren between the ages of one and nine). She always looked forward to these gatherings in their spacious and gracious family home—the same home that also doubled as the town's only bed and breakfast for the remainder of the year.

Edith's husband, Charles Ryan, was the pastor of the only remaining church in town, and some people figured that Edith had no choice but to maintain her positive outlook on life for his sake. And considering that church membership was down more than usual, even for this time of year, it probably made sense that Edith would look for the brighter side, if only to bolster her husband's spirits. This was fortunate, since some members of his congregation seemed determined to do just the opposite.

"Have you noticed that Pastor Charlie seems to be slowing down?" Olive Peters said, totally out of the blue, during quilting circle that week. Of course, the only reason she dared to make this comment was because the pastor's good wife had been unable to attend that day. "It just occurred to me that he's getting up there in years."

"Goodness knows, he's been here forever," said her best friend, retired army nurse Helen Johnson. Accustomed to these two rather dominating women, the other quilters simply sewed and listened without commenting.

"I think we should encourage the poor old guy to retire," added Olive, who was pushing sixty herself.

"For his own sake, of course," Helen said.

"And then maybe we could hire someone *more hip*," said Olive as she tried to see well enough to thread her needle. Not that either of these women were very hip, although Helen had recently had a hip replacement. "A younger man might breathe some new life into the pulpit." She squinted her eyes and attempted, for the third time, to thread the pesky needle. "Help the church to grow."

"Yes," agreed Helen. "We need someone who could get the young people more involved."

"And the community too," added Olive. "There are plenty of folks who don't go to church around here. We should be getting them to come to our church. Membership is way down this year."

"Maybe if we found someone with a more contemporary worldview," inserted Helen. "We all know that Pastor Charlie is a good man, but he can be a bit old-fashioned, don't you think?"

Naturally, Edith's good friend Polly Emery, also present at the quilting circle, kept her thoughts to herself, since she knew that speaking out would only have resulted in an argument. Then the quilt would never get finished in time for Christmas, and it was meant to be a gift for a needy family in town. But she did inform Edith about the dissenters when the two of them met at the North Pole for coffee the following day.

"I really do hate repeating things like this," she said apologetically after spilling her proverbial beans. "But I just thought you should be aware of the talk, Edith. For Charles's sake, you know, so you two can watch your backsides, if you know what I mean."

Edith considered Polly's words as strains of "Silver Bells" played over the tinny sound system in the small café. "Well, Charles does turn sixty-five this year," she admitted with a bit of amazement. Sometimes Edith forgot that her husband was nearly ten years her senior. "But I don't see that as so terribly old, not really. And he does seem to get along with the young people . . . don't you think?"

"Of course he does, Edith. And you're right, Charles seems much younger than his age. Besides, it's not his fault that the young people can't stick around to go to church here. Everyone knows that most of them are forced to leave town to find *real* work. It's not as if we have great career opportunities here in Christmas Valley."

Edith sighed. "Speaking of young people . . . I just found out that not a single one of our kids will be coming home for Christmas this year."

Polly looked shocked. "Really? How can that be? I mean, I realize that Tommy and Alicia and their kids wouldn't be able to make it since they just got stationed in Germany. And you did mention that Katie and her family might not be able to make the trip from Florida this year. But what about Jack and his new wife—what's her name?"

"Constance."

"Right. What about them? I thought they were coming."

"Constance just decided that they should spend Christmas with her parents this year. And, really, that seems only fair. After all, Jack brought her here last Christmas when they got engaged. Remember?"

"What about Krista then? I happen to know that teachers get nearly two weeks off this year, and she only lives in Seattle—she could easily drive here in just a few hours. What's her excuse?"

"Well, that's the thing. She just called this morning, and it seems that she and some teacher friends got the chance to share a condo in Hawaii during the holidays—an opportunity of a lifetime for her. . . . Of course, she had to go."

"Oh . . ." Polly appeared stumped now.

"So it's just Charles and me this year."

"I'd invite you to join us, but we promised Candy and Bill that we'd come to their house this year. We plan to be gone for a whole week."

Edith reached over and patted her friend's hand. "Don't you worry about us, Polly. We'll be just fine."

But as Edith walked home, she wasn't so sure. How could it possibly be Christmas with no kids, no grandkids, no happy voices, no pitter-patter of feet going up and down the stairs, no sticky fingerprints to wipe from the big bay window, no wide-eyed expectations as the little ones tried to guess what Santa might be bringing them this year?

How could it be Christmas with nothing but quiet emptiness filling up their big old Victorian house? Why, it just didn't seem possible. It just wasn't right!

So, despite the tall, fully decorated tree in the center of town and the big red-and-white candy cane decorations on every street lamp . . . despite the life-size Santa's-sleigh-and-reindeer stage in the parking lot next to the Oh, Christmas Tree gift shop and despite all the evergreen wreaths and garlands and strings of little white lights around every shop window and roofline . . . well, it just didn't feel one bit like Christmas knowing that her family wouldn't be coming home this year.

Edith glanced up at the cloudless blue sky overhead and realized that the temperature must be approaching the sixties today, and the weather didn't feel one bit like Christmas either. And with Christmas less than two weeks away . . . Edith sighed. It was just all wrong.

2

Tonight was midweek service, and as usual, Edith prepared a light meal for Charles and herself. But as they sat at the large dining room table, just the two of them at opposite ends, she decided she could not, or rather she *should* not, inform him that not even one of their children would be coming for Christmas this year. She would have to save that unfortunate news for later. Nor would she tell him, not now and not ever, about what Polly had mentioned earlier today. No, there was just no sense in repeating something like that. Instead she made pleasant small talk about a radio program that she'd listened to this afternoon while baking six loaves of cranberry nut bread—one, still warm, that they were enjoying along with their dinner, the rest to go into the freezer for later use or to give away to those who expected company for the holidays.

"It's hard to believe that it's December already," Charles said as he wiped his mouth with a green-and-red-checked napkin. "I think each year passes more quickly than the last."

"It probably comes with age," she said as she began clearing the table. "They say the older you get the faster the days go."

"Need any help?" he offered, just like usual.

And, just like usual—for a Wednesday, that is—she said, "Not tonight, dear. You just go to your study and relax a bit . . . get yourself into the right state of mind for your sermon tonight."

He pecked her on the cheek and thanked her for dinner, then went off on his way while she rinsed the dishes and loaded them into the dishwasher. With its red gingham wallpaper and golden wood floors topped with colorful braided rugs, her kitchen was quite a cheerful place—her own private retreat—

and she never minded spending time there. Whether it was baking or cleaning or sitting at her little maple desk in the corner, this was her territory, and everyone knew it. She even had a sign posted over the door, politely warning guests that this area was "off-limits."

Not that it would be much of a problem during the next two weeks, for as usual, Edith had been careful not to book guests during the weeks before and following Christmas—those were always reserved for family members. And also as usual, the first two weeks of December had been fairly quiet as well. Other than the nice elderly couple who'd just left yesterday, she had no bookings lined up. She figured this was because people were too absorbed with their own holiday preparations to plan an overnight getaway during this busy time.

In the past, she'd always welcomed this quiet lull, kind of like a little reprieve before things got too frantic and chaotic with all the family members arriving, combined with the comings and goings of Christmas in town and at church. But not this year. This year there would be nothing but quiet, quiet, quiet, at least around this house. And as Edith dried her hands on a hand towel embroidered with bright sprigs of holly and berries, she just wasn't sure that she could handle that much quiet.

She heard the front door open and close, the sign that Charles was heading over to the church now, just across the street from their house. He always went over early to turn on the lights and adjust the fussy furnace and, of course, to pray for the service as well as his congregation. Charles had always been a firm believer in prayer. As was Edith, and despite her heavy heart, she took a few minutes to sit down at her desk and bow her head and earnestly pray, first of all for Charles's sermon—that God would bless his words as well as the listeners who heard them—and second that God would remind people like Olive and Helen to watch their words a bit more closely.

Certainly, she wanted to say more about that, but she knew it was up to God to decide whether or not to dish out any vengeance for their careless tongues. Then she pulled on her favorite wool sweater—no need for a coat on this unseasonably warm evening— and headed over to the church herself. Now this was the truth: although she was completely devoted to Charles and never missed a service without an extremely good excuse, there were times, like tonight, when she might've opted to stay home—if that were an option. Which it was not. And perhaps that was a good thing too. Perhaps an encouraging pre-Christmas sermon was just what she needed tonight. Something to help her get back into the *real* spirit of Christmas.

She paused on the sidewalk in front of their house, smiling with satisfaction as she looked across the street and admired the church's colorful stained glass windows glowing so warmly, so invitingly in the velvety night. She remembered the time when the windows were so badly deteriorated that the board had voted to have them completely removed and replaced with pastel-colored bubble glass, the same kind that was used in shower doors! Well, Edith couldn't bear to see that happen, and so she had rallied some women into a fund-raising frenzy, with bake sales and silent auctions until finally, contributing the difference secretly from her own personal savings, enough funds were collected to preserve those dear old windows. *Such a pretty little church*, she thought as she crossed the street. *Such a nice addition to their town.*

She thought back to when she and Charles had arrived at Christmas Valley, back in the sixties. It had been his first assignment after becoming ordained. They were so young and full of hope. Of course, things didn't always go smoothly, and living in a small town could certainly be a challenge. They quickly discovered how a church could easily be split open by things like gossip or jealousy or greed. They had gone through their own congregational trials and had also sadly witnessed other churches that floundered and eventually failed. But there was little to be done about it. As a result, they had wholeheartedly invested themselves in their church, as well as their family and their community—and all things considered, it had paid off well, since there was no place on earth where either of them would rather live out the rest of their days than right here.

Still, it got her goat when people like Helen and Olive went around saying that Charles was "getting too old." *Lord knows those women aren't exactly spring chickens themselves*, she thought as she walked up the stone stairs and reached for the bronze handle on the big wooden door.

"Hello, Edith," trilled a familiar voice from behind her. Edith turned in time to see her old friend Mrs. Fish standing at the bottom of the stairs. Mrs. Fish had taught fifth grade to both Tommy and Jack before retiring years ago, and now Edith estimated she must be in her nineties, although she kept her exact age secret.

"Hello," Edith called back as she retraced her steps down the stairs and, gently placing her hand under the elderly woman's elbow, helped her to slowly ascend the stairs. "Isn't it a lovely evening tonight?"

"Feels like springtime to these old bones."

Edith laughed. "Not very Christmas-like though."

"Who could know for sure?" said Mrs. Fish when they reached the top step. "Perhaps the good Lord saw fit to warm up the Holy Lands when his son was born that night."

Edith considered this as she held the door open. "You could be right, Mrs. Fish. I guess I never thought of it like that."

Mrs. Fish removed her gloves, daintily placed them in her smooth leather purse, and looked back up. "That's probably be-cause so many people assume that Christ-mas and snow are one and the same, Edith.

But the Bible doesn't specify what sort of weather they actually had on that night when our Savior was born, now does it?"

Edith nodded. "Now that I think about it, I'm sure that you must be right, Mrs. Fish."

Mrs. Fish smiled back. She was accustomed to being right. "Just the same, I *do* enjoy a white Christmas," she said.

"A *white* Christmas?" said Helen Johnson, coming from the vestibule on the right. "I hardly think so. The ten-day forecast was for fair skies and sunshine."

"Well, you never know," said Edith, although she wasn't sure that she much cared one way or another, now that her family wouldn't be around to enjoy it. Oh, how the children, even the grown ones, loved going to One Tree Hill for sledding! They would bundle up in layers of scarves, mittens, and hats, and she would make several thermoses of hot cocoa along with a large tin of sugar cookies, and Charles would build a big bonfire down at the bottom of the hill to warm up by. It was such fun. Well, perhaps it would be just as well if no snow flew this year.

Edith found her regular seat, second row on the left, next to the aisle, and sat down, waiting for the service to begin. The mid-week service was always rather small, generally not more than twenty people in all—only the most devout or those who wished to appear so. Edith watched as Marie Williams made her way to the organ. Marie had shown up in Christmas Valley nearly twenty years ago, after her husband had suddenly died while they were on the road looking for work. Broke and in need of employment, Marie was hired by Edith to help with housework, but when Edith discovered that Marie played the organ, she enticed Charles to hire her on as the church organist. Of course, they couldn't afford to pay her much, but Marie said she would've gladly played for free. Still a young and attractive woman (she had been in her twenties back then), it wasn't long before Marie married one of the town's most eligible bachelors, Arnie Williams. And although she no longer needed the job as church organist, she continued to play for all these years out of pure love and loyalty.

Edith leaned back into the pew, relaxing as she listened to the soothing sound of Marie's gifted fingers moving gracefully over the keyboard. Ah, what would they do without her? It wasn't long before Charles made his way to the front of the church and up to the pulpit. As usual, he greeted everyone, made a comment on the warmer than normal weather, and then repeated a humorous story that he'd read in *Reader's Digest* (his favorite source for jokes and anecdotes). The congregation laughed politely, and then he led them in a song and began his sermon. Just like usual.

But, not a bit like usual, Edith was distracted with her own dismal thoughts about how Christmas would not be the same, and how, without her children, it would be bleak and sad. Consequently, she missed the entire first half of her husband's sermon— something she hadn't done since the time when Krista, at the age of six, had pulled out her loose front tooth and bled all over Edith's best blue suit in the middle of a midweek service.

However, when Edith realized that she hadn't been listening to a single word her good husband had been saying, feeling like a child who'd been caught sleeping during mathematics, she sat up straighter and adjusted her gaze directly ahead and even smiled, ever so slightly. Hopefully, Charles hadn't noticed her little faux pas. He certainly had her undivided attention now!

"Our Lord reminded his disciples to show hospitality. He said there could be times when they might help or bless a stranger and in reality be blessing him. Be mindful of this as so many of you open your homes to family and loved ones and life becomes somewhat hectic. Perhaps it is in those moments, when all is not going smoothly and well, perhaps that is the very moment when you might discover the Lord is right there in your midst."

Edith leaned forward just slightly, a bit dismayed at the irony of her husband speaking of hospitality and opening up one's home while their own home would be noticeably empty this year. Of course, he wasn't aware of this yet.

"But will you be ready?" he said now, looking earnestly over his listeners. "Will your heart be ready to greet our Lord? Let me read a passage from Hebrews 13:1–2," he continued as he opened his new leather Bible. Charles had recently purchased a somewhat nontraditional Bible version and had even started using it during his sermons. Edith wasn't sure what church members would think of this modern translation since they were more accustomed to the old-fashioned and traditional Bibles, but so far no one had commented or complained. Perhaps no one had even noticed.

" 'Stay on good terms with each other,' " he read slowly, putting emphasis on each word, " 'held together by love.' " He paused, adjusted his bifocals, and smiled at the congregation. "Isn't that just beautiful? *Held together by love.*" Then he continued to read. "And then it says, 'Be ready with a meal or a bed when it's needed. Why, some have extended hospitality to angels without ever knowing it!' "

Edith listened as he continued to expound on this idea of getting along with each other, encouraging the congregation to outdo each other in the areas of love and hospitality. It really was a perfect pre-Christmas theme, especially in regard to some of the less than loving and slightly divisive comments that Olive and Helen had made earlier this week. Now Edith wondered if Charles hadn't been aware of this all along. Naturally, he wouldn't have mentioned it.

But Edith put thoughts of Olive and Helen aside as she listened to his words. And then, just as she normally did, she began to apply those meaningful words to the state of her own heart, and by the time he finished his sermon and Marie was back at the organ, Edith had tears running down both cheeks. So it was that Edith knew exactly what needed to be done!

3

After the service ended, Edith made an effort at congeniality with fellow parishioners, but all she could think was that she wanted to get home as quickly as possible. Or as her old grandmother might've once said, Edith had a bee in her bonnet.

"Yes, Olive," she said with as much patience as she could muster, "the nativity costumes are still up in the attic." She wanted to add "just like they always have been," but instead she said, "Come on over and get them anytime you like." Olive had taken it upon herself to head up the church's annual nativity play this year. For the past ten years her daughter Judy had managed this challenging task, but Judy and her husband had relocated to Portland last year, and Olive had promised to handle the program for her. Edith just hoped, for the sake of the church, that Olive was up to it.

"I'll give you a call this week," said Olive as she jotted down something in a little black notebook.

"You're certainly organized," observed Edith.

Olive smiled, perhaps a bit smugly. "Judy explained her whole system to me. It's really quite brilliant, if I do say so myself."

Edith patted Olive on the arm. "I sure do miss Judy. She did such a great job with the children and Sunday school. How does she like Portland?"

Olive made a face. "Not very much, I'm afraid. She says the traffic is horrible. If it weren't for Ron's job, I'm sure they'd be back here in no time. But at least they'll all be here for Christmas. And I don't want her to be disappointed in the nativity play. Goodness gracious, but I've got a lot to do!"

Edith considered offering to help, but only for a second or two. She knew that Olive had certain ways of doing things, and in all likelihood Edith would only get in her way. Besides that, Edith was still not completely over Olive's less than kind comments about Charles's age. Maybe managing the nativity play on her own would remind her that they were all getting up there in years, and that it didn't hurt to lean on each other a bit, or to cut each other a bit of grace from time to time—something like tonight's sermon. Edith simply smiled and said she'd better be getting home now.

She waved a little good-bye to Charles, who was caught in what looked like an interesting conversation between Mrs. Fish and Peter Simpson. Peter had gone to school with their boys but somehow managed to eke out a living as an artist and part-time handyman here in town. If memory served her right, he'd also been in Mrs. Fish's class before she retired. Edith was slightly curious as to what the three of them were talking about in such an animated fashion, but she was also eager to get home.

She hurried across the street and into the house, heading straight for her little desk in the kitchen. Without even taking off her sweater, she turned on her computer and sat down, waiting for the screen to come to life. Funny, how she'd fought against the idea of owning a computer—so technical and impersonal—but eventually her children got to her. "How will we keep in touch?" demanded Katie after having her first baby several years ago. "If you had a computer, we could e-mail each other every day, and I'd even send photos of the baby that you could see immediately."

Well, that settled it. And the next time Tommy had a couple of days to spare, he helped his mother to set up a computer and even gave her some beginner lessons— mostly how to turn it off and on and how to play Spider Solitaire, which still probably occupied far too much of her time. But after a while, she had the good sense to get some serious computer tutoring from Jared Renwick, a local teen who was also a computer whiz. She eventually got the hang of it, and now, thanks to Jared, who had recently started his own small computer business, she even had a website for the bed and breakfast that could be accessed by people from all over the world. Amazing, really.

She emailed Jared now. "Dear Jared," she carefully typed, still using the formal and, according to her children, "old-fashioned" greeting. They usually just wrote "Hey Mom" or sometimes launched right into their latest news without a proper heading. But she still liked to start all email correspondence with "Dear"—it just seemed polite.

Dear Jared,
    I've just come up with a promotion idea that I'd like you to display on my website, that is if you're not too busy. I want to announce that for the first time in the seventeen years of its operation, the Shepherd's Inn will be open throughout the entire month of December. And also that, as a Christmas special, I will be offering a 25 percent discount to all guests. Plus, all guests will be included in all the Christmas activities at no additional cost, including the Christmas Eve party and Christmas dinner and so on. Can you please take care of this for me?
    Sincerely,
    Edith Ryan

Then Edith hit the magical "send" button and returned to her currently empty e-mail in-box and waited expectantly. Well, she didn't really think he'd get back to her immediately, but sometimes he was a regular Johnny-on-the-spot. Still, when he didn't respond after a couple of minutes, she decided to distract herself with a quick game of Spider Solitaire. What could it hurt? But before she'd even dealt the second row of cards, she heard the familiar little *bing-bing* sound, announcing that new mail had arrived. And sure enough, it was from Jared.

no problem, E. done deal. jr

She smiled to herself as she signed off, then shut down her computer. Despite his computer "shorthand," Edith knew that Jared had taken care of everything. Just like that. Now, didn't they live in an amazing era! Hopefully, she'd get some responses to her Christmas special by the end of the week. Guests, as instructed on the website, e-mailed or called Edith directly to book rooms, and she hoped that they'd have all five rooms booked by the weekend. Or at least some of them—perhaps it wasn't imperative to have a full house, although that would be her preference. And who knew what kind of interesting guests they might have during the holidays. Perhaps like Charles had said tonight, they might even entertain angels or the Lord himself without ever knowing it.

She hummed to herself as she puttered in the kitchen, putting on the kettle for their nightly cup of tea, and as she measured the tea she imagined the sorts of people who might book rooms during the holidays. Perhaps there would be some older couples who, like Edith and Charles, didn't have family to gather with this year. Or maybe a young family who'd recently relocated from the East Coast, finding themselves without relatives nearby. Well, Edith and Charles could become their temporary family! And they would show their guests the best sort of hospitality that a place like Christmas Valley had to offer. Really, it would be such fun! Perhaps it truly was a blessing in disguise that her children were unable to come this year. It would give her the opportunity to really reach out to people who might otherwise have a sad and lonely Christmas. A chance to practice real hospitality—just the way the good Lord intended. She couldn't wait to tell Charles about her plan!

The kettle was just beginning to sing

when Charles came into the kitchen. Edith turned and smiled at her husband. "I have a surprise for you!"

At first Charles, like she had been, was dismayed to hear that none of their children would be coming home for Christmas, but she quickly moved into the second part of her surprise, and before long his eyes lit up too.

"That's wonderful, dear," he said as he set his mug of orange pekoe tea down on the small kitchen table. "You may be the only one who actually took my little sermon seriously."

"What do you mean?"

He waved his hand in a dismissive way. "Oh, nothing, really."

"What?" she insisted, leaning forward to listen.

"Oh, I think that some members of our congregation may think that angels are an antiquated old fairy tale."

She frowned. "That's too bad."

He nodded. "Yes. Mrs. Fish is certain that angels only visited the biblical characters, not modern-day people like us." He shook his head. "And Peter Simpson believes that angels are simply metaphorical, symbols of God's attempt to reach mankind, or something to that effect."

"Oh . . ."

Charles shrugged. "I was beginning to feel that I'm a bit out of touch with my parishioners."

Edith didn't speak, but she was considering what Polly had told her about Helen and Olive and their concern that Charles was getting old.

Then her husband smiled. "But now I come home to discover that my own dear wife has taken my words to heart." He reached over and put his hand on hers. "That is a great comfort."

"It's a comfort to me too," she said. "I was so discouraged to think that our kids weren't coming. It just didn't seem like Christmas."

"I wonder who the Lord will bring to our home," he mused. "Perhaps we should take a few minutes to pray about this, Edith, to invite our Lord to direct the right people to us—the ones who need a bit of Christmas Valley cheer and hospitality to warm their hearts. Do you think?"

She nodded and bowed her head, and together they asked God to guide the perfect people to the Shepherd's Inn for the holidays.

"Isn't it exciting?" she said when they finished.

He squeezed her hand and nodded. "Yes, dear, it is!"

But the next day came, and not one phone call, not one e-mail had arrived by the afternoon. Even so, Edith busied herself with the same sort of preparations she would do when expecting her family to fill the house. She even called Polly to tell her of the plan.

"What a great idea," said Polly, who had missed Charles's midweek sermon the night before. Edith explained where the inspiration came from, and Polly said she wished she could be around to watch what happened.

"I'll tell you all about it when you get back," said Edith.

"So have you had any bites yet?"

"Not yet," said Edith in her optimistic way. "But it hasn't even been twenty-four hours since Jared changed my website. I'm sure they will come."

"Yes, of course," said Polly, but Edith thought she heard a tinge of doubt in her friend's voice.

"And if they don't," said Edith, "well, I'll just do like the good Lord says. I'll go out to the streets and invite strangers to come in."

"Really?" Polly sounded a bit shocked now.

"Well, I don't know for sure, Polly. I can't

imagine there would be many strangers roaming the streets of Christmas Valley right at Christmastime." She laughed. "But you just never know!"

4

On Friday morning the phone rang, and it turned out to be a woman named Carmen Fields from Redding, California. She had just found the Shepherd's Inn website.

"Do you still have rooms available?" she asked hopefully.

"Yes, we do," said Edith, not wanting to admit that *all* the rooms were currently available.

"Well, my husband and I decided that we'd like to do something different for Christmas this year," she said. "And it seems that everyone else in our family has plans." She cleared her throat. "Plans that don't include us."

"Well, we would love to *include* you with us," said Edith happily. Then she took down the pertinent information and booked the room. "And there's a nice website for the town," she informed Carmen. "It tells a bit about us and some of the activities that happen around here at Christmastime."

"Sounds perfect," said Carmen. "We plan to drive up, take our time, and spend a night somewhere along the way. So I guess we'll see you on Monday then."

Edith smiled to herself as she hung up the phone. It was starting to happen. *A real beginning!* And, remembering her wise husband's suggestion on Wednesday night, Edith took a few moments to ask God, once again, to send just the right people to their home. She also thanked him for choosing Carmen and Jim Fields and even asked his blessing on their travels as they made their way up here by car.

By noon on Saturday, Edith had booked two more rooms. One was for a single man named Albert Benson. Judging by his voice, he was older and, Edith guessed, sad. Although she had no reason why. No matter, they would do whatever possible to cheer him up during his stay. The next booking was done online. A couple from Spokane by the name of Lauren and Michael Thomas, just the two of them. No children yet. Oh, well, Edith assured herself, God was in control of the guest list, and it wasn't for her to question.

But later in the afternoon she received a call from a woman named Leslie. "I have a child," she began tentatively, "a five-year-old daughter. . . . I hope that's okay."

"That's wonderful!" said Edith. "I was just hoping that someone would have children. It just feels more like Christmas with little ones around."

"Her name is Megan, and she's still having a hard time adjusting to the fact that her daddy left us more than a year ago. . . ."

"Oh, I'm so sorry."

"Don't be. The guy was a total jerk. The only good thing he ever did for me was Megan. But for some reason she still thinks he's the greatest and doesn't understand why he can't come spend Christmas with us. Anyway, I needed someplace to go . . . to get away from here, you know what I mean?"

"Well, you and Megan are more than welcome to make yourselves at home here," said Edith.

"Great. I'm taking the whole week off, so I plan to drive over on Tuesday. Is that okay?"

"No problem."

And so it was that all but one room was booked. Edith was busier than ever now, but it was just the way she liked it. Naturally, she'd sent her Christmas cards weeks ago and had, just last week, finished wrapping and shipping her children's Christmas presents, but she still had plenty to do to make her guests feel completely welcome and at home here. She was just carrying a load of clean towels upstairs when she heard the doorbell ring. Setting the basket on a chair, she turned and hurried back down. Too early for guests to be arriving, thank goodness. She opened the door to see Olive Peters standing there.

"I tried to call, but your line was busy," she explained. "I came to collect the costumes. We're going to do a fitting this afternoon."

Feeling more generous than the last time they'd talked, Edith offered to help her carry the boxes over to the church.

"Oh, I don't want to bother you," said

Olive, impatiently looking at her watch. "And Helen promised to help me, but as usual, she's late."

"Why don't I give you a hand?"

"Oh, I'm sure you've got your hands full. Aren't you busy getting ready for all those kids of yours to arrive?"

So Edith explained how things were going to be different this year.

"You've got to be kidding!" exclaimed Olive. "You and Charles must've lost your minds."

Edith blinked. "Why—what do you mean?"

"Inviting a bunch of perfect strangers into your home during Christmas?"

"Well, I do run a bed and breakfast," said Edith. "We're accustomed to having strangers as guests—"

"But for Christmas, Edith?" Olive firmly shook her head. "It just sounds a little odd. Christmas is a time for friends and family. If you and Charles were going to be alone during the holidays, you should've told us. We would've gladly invited you over to our home. You shouldn't be stuck here with a bunch of strangers."

Edith forced what she hoped was a believable smile. "But that's just it, Olive, we *want* to do this. Don't you remember Charles's midweek sermon about being hospitable? We wanted to open our home to people who don't have a place to go during this time. We thought it would be fun."

Olive pressed her lips together and studied Edith for a long moment. "Well, all I can say is that you two have a very strange idea of what constitutes *fun*. And I certainly hope that this whole crazy plan doesn't backfire and blow up in your face."

Just then Helen drove up, and Edith was relieved that she was now off the hook for helping Olive with the costumes. She led the two women up the two flights of stairs, then turned around in concern to Helen. "Oh, my, I hope this doesn't hurt your hip," she said. "I forgot all about your surgery."

"No problem," huffed Helen, clearly out of breath. "That replacement hip," *gasp gasp*, "is as good as new."

"But I might need one now," said Olive just as breathlessly. It seemed that she too was trying to recover from climbing the two flights of stairs. "Or maybe I should focus on my knees first. They've been giving me trouble lately."

Edith opened the door to the attic and

turned on the light. "I'll warn you that it's very dusty up here," she said as she led them over to the corner where the cardboard boxes of costumes were stored.

"All *six* of these?" exclaimed Olive when she saw the clearly marked boxes. "For one little nativity play?"

"That means more trips," said Helen with a frown. "You didn't warn me that I was signing up for hard labor today, Olive."

Olive went over and picked up a box. "Well, at least they're not terribly heavy." Without commenting, Helen followed her lead. Edith, deciding not to waste a trip down the stairs, picked up a box herself, the largest one as it turned out, and it was a bit on the heavy side.

By the time they were all downstairs, both Helen and Olive looked thoroughly winded, but they somehow managed to get out the door and were slowly making their way over to the church when Charles poked his head out of his study. "What's going on?"

Edith explained about the costume boxes, and before the two women had a chance to return, Charles had retrieved the other three from the attic and was already carrying two of the boxes across the street. Edith smiled as she watched him. Maybe this would give Helen and Olive something to think about. Maybe witnessing Charles's ability to carry the boxes without being the least bit out of breath, since, regardless of the weather, he regularly walked two miles every morning, would show those ladies that he wasn't exactly over the hill yet.

"Those two," he said when he came back into the house. "I'll be surprised if the pageant doesn't turn into a complete fiasco."

"Really?" Edith looked at him with concern. "Do you think they're going to make a mess of it?"

He laughed. "Oh, probably not. After all, as Olive assured me, she does have her little notebook, her attack plan . . . that should keep the affair somewhat on target. But the way those two were arguing just now, about who was boss and who was going to do what, well, I just hope they don't set too bad of an example for the children."

"I do miss Judy," said Edith.

"We all do."

"And I know this sounds terrible, but sometimes it's difficult to believe that Judy and Olive are actually related."

He laughed again. "Hopefully, Judy won't

be too disappointed when they get here and see what's become of her pageant."

"Maybe she'll be able to save the day."

Just then the doorbell rang again.

"This place is like Grand Central Station today," observed Charles. "I hope I'll be able to get my sermon finished."

"Don't worry," she assured him. "It's probably just Olive and Helen again. Anyway, whatever it is, I'll take care of it. You get back to your work, dear."

But it wasn't Olive or Helen. Instead, Edith found a short and rather squat woman standing at her door. The woman's hair was gray and fluffy, and she appeared to be quite elderly. At least eighty or ninety, Edith suspected.

"Can I help you?" she asked the woman, who didn't look one bit happy to be there.

"I suppose you can. My friend just dropped me off here." She looked over her shoulder and scowled. "You got any room in your inn?"

Edith blinked. "Someone dropped you off? Right here? And you need a room?"

"That's what I said, isn't it? You got a room or not?" The old woman shifted her shabby-looking overnight bag to the other hand and sighed in clear exasperation. "You're not deaf, are you?"

"No, of course not." Edith opened the door wider. "Please, come in."

"Well, that's better." The woman shoved the overnight bag toward Edith as if she were a bellboy.

Without questioning this, Edith took the bag and led the woman over to the long oak table that she used as a registration area, setting the bag down on the chair beside it. She wasn't quite sure what to say now.

"Come on," said the old woman impatiently. "Cat got your tongue?"

"No . . ." Edith studied the woman. Something about her reminded Edith of Ulysses, a bulldog that had belonged to her grandfather when she was a little girl. Maybe it was the square, flat face, or the loose jowls, or perhaps it was something in those intense, slightly beady eyes. But Edith had never quite trusted that dog.

"Well, then . . . what's the problem?"

Still, Edith didn't like to judge people on appearances. "I'm sorry, but people usually call ahead first, to get reservations, and I'm just caught a little off—"

"Look, if you're booked up just tell me, and I'll get out of your hair."

"No," Edith said quickly. Perhaps a bit too quickly. "We do actually have an available room."

"Fine," snapped the woman. "I'll take it."

"Right," said Edith, still trying to grasp what was going on. She hated to be rude, but she really wanted to know why this woman had decided to come here of all places. It wasn't as if they were exactly on the beaten path. Just the same, she slid the information form toward the woman. "You'll just need to fill this out for me."

"You mind if I sit down?" demanded the woman. "My feet are killing me."

"No, not at all," said Edith, removing the bag from the chair and offering the woman a seat. "I'm curious as to how you heard about us."

"My friend knew where you were located. It was his idea to drop me here. I s'pect he didn't want me around during the holidays." She made a disgusted sigh. "Nice friend, huh?"

Just then the doorbell rang again. "Excuse me," said Edith as she went to get it.

It was Olive, and her face looked a bit

stricken. "I need your help, Edith. Helen slipped on a wet spot on the floor in the kitchen, and she can't get up."

"Oh, my goodness," said Edith. "Is she badly hurt?"

"I don't think so. She told me not to call 911. But I'm not strong enough to get her up by myself. As you know, Helen is a rather bulky gal."

Edith looked back at the old woman. "If you'll excuse me for just a few minutes, I need to—"

"I heard the whole stupid thing," snapped the woman without even turning to see them. "I'll be perfectly fine on my own. It's not as if I'm not used to it, for Pete's sake."

Olive's brows lifted curiously at this.

"I'll be right back," called Edith as she headed for the door. "Come on, Olive."

"Who is *that*?" demanded Olive as soon as the door was shut behind them.

"I'm not exactly sure," said Edith. "Well, she's a guest, of course, but I didn't get her name yet."

"There you go," said Olive as if making a point. "Letting a perfect stranger into your house, you don't even know her name, on top of that she's ruder than all get-out. . . .

The next thing you know she'll be making off with the family silver."

Edith laughed. "We don't have much silver, Olive. And I seriously doubt that she could carry much with her. She looks like she's about a hundred years old. Someone just dumped her here, poor thing."

"*Dumped* her?"

"Well, dropped her. She said it was a friend."

"Some friend."

"That's what she said too."

They were in the church now, and the sounds of moaning made Edith hasten her pace. There in the small church kitchen, just like Olive had said, was Helen Johnson lying flat as a pancake with arms and legs sprawled out like a beached starfish.

"Are you okay?" asked Edith as she knelt down beside her and attempted to remember what she'd learned at her first aid class, more than twenty years ago.

"You mean other than being in severe pain and humiliating embarrassment?" said Helen.

"Can you move everything?" asked Edith, recalling that you weren't supposed to attempt transporting someone with a spinal injury.

"What would you suggest that I move?"

"You know," said Edith. "Your arms and your legs, does everything work okay?"

Now Helen waved her arms and legs as if she were making a snow angel.

"Okay," said Edith, satisfied. "It looks like you're pretty much in one piece. Can you sit up?"

"Perhaps with a little help."

Neither Edith nor Olive was particularly large or muscular, so Edith took one hand and Olive took the other, and together they pulled Helen to a sitting position.

"How's that?" asked Edith.

"Better." Helen rubbed her knee. "Although I do feel a bit foolish."

Edith went for a wooden chair now. She thought it might be a better way to help Helen to her feet.

"You shouldn't feel bad, Helen," said Olive. "It's that ding-dong janitor who's to blame. He shouldn't have left a wet spot on the floor like that. A person could get killed taking a fall like that."

"He probably didn't realize anyone was

going to be here today," said Edith as she set the chair next to Helen.

"What's that for?" asked Helen.

"I thought we could use it to help you get up," suggested Edith. "Olive and I can each lift you from the sides, and maybe you can help to hoist yourself up with the chair."

"Well, as long as you can keep the chair from slipping," said Helen a bit skeptically. So they all got into place, and before long they had Helen on her feet, then sitting in the chair.

"Thank you, girls," said Helen. "I suppose it's time to consider having some work done on these old knees of mine. This right one is really howling now."

"That's what I keep telling you," said Olive. "Get yourself fixed up while you can. We're not getting any younger, you know."

"Are you going to be okay?" asked Edith.

Helen attempted standing now, holding on to each of them as she did. "My hip is okay, but my knee's a bit sore. I'm sure that's partly due to going up and down all those stairs earlier. But I doubt that I'm going to be much help to you today," she told Olive.

"Why don't we help you to your car," suggested Edith. "Do you think you can drive okay?"

"Of course," said Helen, ever the stalwart army nurse. "And if someone calls ahead, Clarence can help me into the house when I get there."

"I'll do that," said Edith.

So the three of them slowly hobbled off toward Helen's Crown Victoria, which was parked close to the side exit from the church kitchen. Thankfully, that meant no stairs. They finally had Helen in her car, and she thanked them once again.

"I'm sorry I can't help you," she told Olive.

"It's quite all right, dear," said Olive, glancing at her watch. "Goodness, the kids will be here any minute. I better get moving."

"Take care," said Edith. "And I'll give Clarence a call right now."

"Appreciate it."

"Let me know if you need a hand today," Edith called to Olive as she was hurrying back to the church.

"I think you have your hands full with grandma over there," said Olive. Then she paused. "But thanks anyway. I think I can handle this on my own."

Edith was relieved to hear this, and as a matter of fact, she was a bit concerned, not to mention curious, about the old woman whom she'd left behind at the registration table. But when she got inside the house, there was no one to be seen. Everything was quiet, and for a moment she wondered if perhaps she'd imagined the whole thing. But then why would Olive have mentioned it?

She decided to peek her head into Charles's study to see if he knew anything. "Sorry to disturb you, dear," she began.

He looked up from where he was intently writing. "Yes?"

"Uh, did you happen to see an old woman anywhere about—"

He adjusted his glasses and peered at her. "You mean *Myrtle*?"

"Well, I'm not totally sure." Edith held out her hand to about four and a half feet high. "She was about this tall"—now she spread her arms—"and about this wide."

He kind of smiled. "I think you must mean our guest. Myrtle Pinkerton."

She nodded. "Our guest?"

"She filled out her paperwork and paid for two full weeks in advance—with cash, by the way; I put it in your little zipper bag—so I could see no reason not to take her to a room. I gave her the Green Meadow Room. Is that okay?" All the guest rooms had names related to shepherds, all taken from the twenty-third psalm. There was, of course, the Good Shepherd Room, the Lamb Room, the Staff and Rod Room (which usually had to be explained), the Cool Water Room, and the Green Meadow Room.

Edith smiled. "That's fine, dear. And thank you for helping out when I know you're busy."

"And is everyone okay over at the church?"

"Yes." She wanted to let him get back to his work now. "Everyone's just fine."

"Myrtle mentioned that someone had fallen down and couldn't get up." His eyes twinkled with curiosity. "But she didn't seem to think it was an actual emergency."

"Yes, that was Helen." Edith decided to give him the sweet, condensed version for the time being. "She slipped, but she's okay. Olive and I got her up and into her car. Don't worry about it. I'll try not to disturb you again."

He smiled. "I can hardly blame you for Helen's fall, dear."

She nodded and quietly pulled the door closed.

Goodness, how did this day get so busy?

5

"I thought this was a bed and *breakfast.*"

Edith looked up from where she was sitting at the kitchen table. Her normal routine was to get up early enough to read from her morning devotional book and enjoy a quiet cup of peppermint tea. Her private time. But Myrtle Pinkerton, ignoring the sign above the door, had just stepped over an invisible line and was now standing with a bulldoggish expression as she surveyed Edith's kitchen.

Edith slowly closed her book, glanced at the apple-shaped clock above the stove to see that it wasn't yet 6:00 a.m., then cleared her throat and stood.

"Good morning, Mrs. Pinkerton," she said in a formal voice. "Perhaps my husband didn't give you our brochure yesterday, but breakfast isn't served until seven. I'm sorry for any inconvenience."

"Hmmph. Inconvenience is right. I'm an old woman. I didn't have any dinner last night, and I am *starving*."

Despite her resolve to maintain her normal professional and cool facade right now (her means for dealing with the occasional cantankerous guest), Edith did feel her sympathetic side taking over once again. Edith's family and friends had often warned her that she was a softie and that if she wasn't careful, everyone would walk all over her. But, for goodness' sake, this poor old woman was virtually stranded at the inn, and although there were a couple of eating establishments in town, they were also several blocks away, and who knew what kind of walking shape Myrtle Pinkerton was in.

"Why don't you make yourself comfortable in the dining room," suggested Edith in a kind voice. "And I'll bring you something out. Do you like tea, Mrs. Pinkerton?"

"No. I only drink coffee. Cream and sugar. And call me Myrtle. I don't go in for formalities." She turned around, made a *harrumph* sound as if she were reluctant to leave, then returned to the dining room.

Edith suppressed feelings of guilt now. Was she being too rigid with this guest? Really, what harm would come from inviting Myrtle to join her in the kitchen just this once? "Don't compromise yourself," she could just hear her children warning her. Or even Polly. "Don't give in, Edith. Stay firm or you'll regret it." Of course, they were probably right.

Edith considered asking Myrtle whether or not she had any special dietary needs but then decided the best course might be to start brewing coffee first. Besides, Charles would be down before long, and he would be pleased to see that the coffee was already made. After a few minutes, she carried a tray with a cup of steaming coffee, along with cream and sugar, to the dining room. But no one was there.

"Myrtle?" she called out, thinking perhaps the guest had wandered into the living room or maybe the sunroom, but no one answered. So she set the tray on the table and returned to the kitchen to begin cutting up some fruit for a small fruit plate. Surely fresh fruit would be a safe choice to start with. She also set out a couple of pitchers of fruit juice. Then she neatly arranged a small plate of sliced cranberry nut bread along with the pumpkin bread she had baked only yesterday. She made toast, got out some jelly, and finally set out a selection of yogurts and cereals to choose from—her usual fare when they had only one or two guests in the house. Of course, guests were welcome to order eggs and other cooked items if they liked, and Edith was always more than happy to turn on the stove, but this lighter fare usually suited most guests just fine.

Still there was no sign of Myrtle. And even when Edith did a quick search of the first-floor rooms, she never found her. Perhaps Myrtle had gone back to her room for something. She waited a bit, but eventually it was only her and Charles, sitting down to breakfast just the two of them. A rather grand breakfast too, since they were accustomed to eating much lighter when no guests were about, often simply oatmeal and juice.

"Did you see Myrtle this morning?" she

asked as she took a slice of pumpkin bread and broke it in half.

"No, I expect she'd be sleeping in. She mentioned that she was worn out from her trip yesterday."

So Edith explained how Myrtle had been up before six and had claimed to be ravenous. She waved at the nicely arranged table. "Otherwise, I wouldn't have gone to such trouble."

"She's a funny old bird, isn't she?"

Edith nodded, then lowered her voice. "I have a feeling she's going to test my patience a bit. Did you really say that she planned to be here for two whole weeks?"

He smiled. "It'll be better when the other guests arrive. Besides, I suspect that poor old Myrtle just needs to be loved."

"Well, perhaps you can take care of that end of things," she suggested. "And I'll take care of the practical things."

He set down his empty coffee cup. "Oh, you can't fool me, Edith. I know you have just as much love to give as I do."

"Well, it didn't feel like that this morning when she was standing in my kitchen and reminding me that this was a bed and *breakfast.*"

He laughed. "This should be an interesting Christmas for everyone."

"Did you invite Myrtle to church when you talked to her yesterday?"

"As a matter of fact, I did."

"And?"

"It sounded as if she plans to come." He wiped his mouth with the napkin. "Speaking of church, I promised Hal Berry that I'd have a short meeting with the ushers this morning. Seems they have some new idea to make things go more smoothly."

"I thought things usually went pretty smoothly." She refilled her cup with tea.

He winked at her. "Well, you know Hal. He's always got some new trick up his sleeve. Remember when he wanted to put the offering plates on sticks so the ushers would have complete control of them at all times?"

She laughed. "Yes, as if there's anyone in our congregation with sticky fingers."

"Well, old Hal isn't quite as trusting as you are, my dear." He bent down and pecked her on the cheek. "See you later."

Edith was just clearing the dining room table when Myrtle made an appearance. She had on a gray woolen coat with an ancient-looking purse slung over one arm. Her cheeks were flushed, and she looked slightly winded.

"Oh, there you are," said Edith as she set the tray back down. "Are you still hungry?"

Myrtle waved one hand and grasped the back of a chair with the other. "No," she puffed. "I just walked all the way to town and back."

"Did you get something to eat?"

She nodded. "I went to that silly café, the one with all the Santa Claus paraphernalia all over the place."

"Mrs. Santa's Diner."

"That's the one. Even the napkins had Santa heads printed all over them. Land sakes, I'd think people would get sick and tired of that Santa stuff day in, day out, year round."

Edith smiled. "Oh, I suppose it gets old for some folks. But I think it's rather charming."

Myrtle released the back of the chair and stood up straighter and said, "Charming? Humph," rolling her eyes for added emphasis.

Edith almost expected her to add a "Bah, humbug" next. But fortunately, Myrtle did not. Instead she turned and began to leave the room.

"I'm going to my room to rest some," she called over her shoulder. "That long walk wore me out something fierce."

"Church is at ten thirty," Edith called out.

Myrtle turned around and tossed her an exasperated look. "I know that," she snapped.

Edith tried not to show her relief as Myrtle slowly made her way toward the staircase. Hopefully, the old woman would enjoy a nice long rest this morning, allowing Edith to get a few more things done without interruption. More guests would begin to arrive tomorrow, and it wouldn't be long before the whole house would be filled. Edith wanted to have everything just perfect for them.

She managed to mix up a batch of sugar cookie dough, which needed to chill, as well as eight pie crusts that she wrapped and stacked in the freezer. She planned to have an assortment of desserts available to her guests throughout the days preceding Christmas. Sweets to cheer the spirits.

Finally it was nearly ten thirty, and Edith knew that it was time to head over to the church. She had neither heard nor seen Myrtle and suspected that the tired old woman might still be soundly sleeping. And perhaps it was for the best. But as Edith made her way down the center aisle, toward her regular seat up front, she was surprised to see that someone was already sitting there. And she suspected, by the gray coat and frazzled-looking hair, not to mention the width that took up a fair portion of pew, that it was indeed Myrtle. Of course, Myrtle would have no idea that she was sitting in the seat that was reserved for the pastor's wife. But Edith could see that the ushers were concerned. She simply smiled at Hal Berry, nodding as if to show him that all was well, before she squeezed past Myrtle, taking the seat to her left. It did feel odd to be sitting in a different spot, even if it was only a few feet different. Funny how people can get accustomed to certain things. Even so, she didn't let on that she was troubled by being bumped from her regular seat. It was silly, really.

After the singing was finished, Charles took a few moments to welcome newcomers. Today that meant Myrtle. He gave a brief introduction, mentioning that she would be staying at the inn throughout the holidays. And then, to Edith's complete surprise and probably everyone else's too, Myrtle stood up.

"Thank you," she said in a loud voice, turning toward the congregation as if preparing to give a speech. "You have an interesting little town here," she continued. "Although I do think you people take this whole Christmas business way too far. Good grief, I actually wiped my mug with Santa faces this morning." A few titters were heard, although Edith suspected that Myrtle wasn't trying to be funny. "What bothers me is that you people are going to forget what Christmas is really about." She shook her finger at them. "It's not about 'Jingle Bells' and candy canes and Santa head toilet-seat covers. It's not about making a few extra bucks or impressing your friends with the way your place is all lit up. And if this is all that Christmas Valley has to offer, well, I'd just as soon spend my Christmas someplace else!" Then she turned and sat down with a *thump*.

The church was so quiet you could have heard a snowflake fall. Not that there was any chance of that today, since it was still quite balmy. Edith, almost afraid to breathe, looked up at the pulpit, where Charles's eyes were wide and his mouth was actually partway open. But he quickly regained composure and even acknowledged Myrtle's stern reprimand.

"I think our guest makes a valid point," he said slowly. "It is important that we not lose sight of the true meaning of Christmas." He smiled. "And I'm sure that's why all of you are here this morning." Then he launched into his sermon.

Unfortunately, Edith was so distracted by Myrtle's strong words, not to mention being deposed from her regular seat, that she was unable to really focus. All she could think of was that this Myrtle had a lot of nerve to dress down the entire congregation. Good grief, she'd been here for less than twenty-four hours, and she was already telling people how to act. It was just a bit much. And, although it wasn't Edith's fault, she felt personally responsible for her guest's less than thoughtful behavior. She couldn't imagine how she was going to make up for it—especially to someone like Olive Peters, and Edith could feel Olive's eyes peering at her from across the church right now.

Finally the service was over, they were singing the anthem, and Edith was considering making a swift exit out the side door in the kitchen. But before she had a chance to make her getaway, someone tapped her on the shoulder from behind.

Edith turned in the pew to see Mrs. Fish. And her old wrinkled face looked concerned.

"I'd like to be introduced to your guest," she said.

But by then Myrtle had already turned around. "I'm Myrtle," she said without fanfare.

Mrs. Fish nodded with a stiff smile.

"This is my friend Mrs. Fish," said Edith quickly. "She's a retired schoolteacher."

Myrtle stuck out her hand. "Nice to meet you."

"I was interested in your comments this morning," began Mrs. Fish.

Then before another word was said, Edith hastily excused herself and made her exit. Oh, she was curious as to what Mrs. Fish was going to say to Myrtle. But not curious enough to stick around. Who knew what might happen with two opinionated women like that. Of course, the ever courteous Mrs. Fish would probably practice perfect self-control. But Myrtle seemed to be a bit of a loose cannon, and Edith didn't care to be around to witness any fireworks. Instead she made her quick getaway as planned, getting all the way to the kitchen before Olive caught up with her.

"Where on earth did that woman come from?" demanded Olive in quiet tones.

Edith smiled. "I'm not sure." Then changing the subject, "How is Helen doing?"

"Helen's fine," Olive said quickly. "But seriously, Edith, what is wrong with that woman? I thought she was going to start preaching fire and brimstone at us. You and Pastor Charles better make sure you keep her in check."

Edith wasn't sure how to respond, but apparently that didn't matter, because now Mrs. Fish and Myrtle were coming into the kitchen.

"I want you to meet Olive Peters," said Mrs. Fish. "Olive?"

Olive looked over with a confused expression. "Yes?"

"Well, Myrtle and I were just discussing the real meaning of Christmas, and she was telling me how she's something of an expert when it comes to nativity productions and such. And I told her that you're managing the pageant this year, and about Helen's fall and how she hurt her knee and won't be of much help." Mrs. Fish smiled. "And it seems you're in luck, Olive. Myrtle just volunteered to give you a hand."

Olive tossed a warning look to Edith, almost as if she expected Edith to remedy this perplexing situation. But Edith was at a complete loss for words at the moment. She just wanted to get back to her kitchen and baking and to forget all about this unpredictable Myrtle Pinkerton.

"When do we start?" asked Myrtle, as if it were all settled.

Olive's lips were pinched tightly together, and Edith actually felt sorry for her.

"I—uh—we're having a rehearsal today," Olive finally said in a flat voice. "It starts at one."

"Maybe we should spend some time planning first," suggested Myrtle. "During lunch works for me." She frowned. "Although I can't say much for the choices of eateries in this town."

Olive cleared her throat. "Well, if you want to come home with me . . . I could warm us up some beef stew that I made last night."

Myrtle nodded. "What are we waiting for?"

Edith smiled to herself as she crossed the street. Olive might've met her match in Myrtle. Hopefully, it wouldn't ruin the Christmas pageant or do any other sort of permanent damage to Christmas or Christmas Valley in general. And it might keep Myrtle occupied and, consequently, out of trouble.

6

"Are you going over to the church to help Olive with the pageant today?" Edith asked Myrtle on Monday morning, hoping that perhaps she'd get a short reprieve from Myrtle's nonstop prattle, most of it focused on how Edith was or was not preparing a recipe correctly. Despite the sign above the kitchen door that clearly stated, Edith had previously believed, that this area was strictly off-limits to guests, Myrtle persisted in coming in and making herself at home. Not only that, she persisted in giving Edith culinary suggestions like, "Shouldn't you add some anise to that batter?" And then when Edith's back was turned, Myrtle took the liberty to add it, generously. Perhaps it would make the cookies taste better, but it irritated Edith just the same.

"The rehearsal isn't until this afternoon," said Myrtle as she poured herself another cup of coffee and watched Edith stirring the dough.

Edith considered reminding Myrtle about her kitchen rule again, but since the past two attempts had clearly fallen upon deaf ears, why waste her breath?

"When are the other Christmas guests coming?" asked Myrtle as she watched Edith starting to roll out cookie dough. Edith had already explained to Myrtle about her children and how they'd been unable to come home for Christmas, and thus her plan for opening her home during the holidays.

"Some are supposed to arrive in the afternoon."

"Here," said Myrtle, suddenly reaching for the rolling pin and actually taking it right from Edith's hands. "Let me show you how it's *supposed* to be done."

Edith watched helplessly as Myrtle took over the menial task that anyone else would've gladly relinquished. But instead

Edith felt irritated. And something else too. Another emotion stirred within her—a feeling she couldn't even name. But something about this whole kitchen scene felt very familiar to her. She just couldn't put her finger on it.

"Have you always lived in Christmas Valley?" asked Myrtle as she skillfully worked the rolling pin over the dough.

Edith decided it probably wouldn't hurt to tell Myrtle the nutshell version of how she and Charles relocated from Iowa after he finished seminary. The whole while she watched, almost mesmerized, as the rolling pin moved steadily back and forth across the dough.

"What about *your* family?"

"You mean my children?"

"No. I mean your parents."

Edith considered this for a long moment, unsure as to how much she wished to disclose to this almost complete stranger, but finally said, "I was raised by my grandparents. They both passed on several years ago."

Myrtle nodded. "Any brothers or sisters?"

"No."

"That must've been pretty lonely for you, growing up . . ."

Edith nodded, somewhat surprised at what seemed a compassionate response from Myrtle. "Yes, I suppose that's one of the reasons that I like having my children around me at Christmastime. It helps to make up for all those quiet Christmases when it was just my grandparents and me."

"You ready?" asked Myrtle, holding up the rolling pin like a torch or maybe a club.

"For what?" Edith felt confused.

"The dough. It's time to cut the cookies."

"Oh."

As Edith and Myrtle proceeded to cut out cookies in the shapes of trees, stars, angels . . . placing them one by one on the buttered cookie sheet, Edith found herself thinking about her childhood. And that's when it occurred to her that Myrtle reminded her a bit of her grandmother. Fairly bossy, pushy, and rather outspoken. Her grandmother had been one of those women who knew it all and wanted everyone around her to know that she did. Oh, Edith had always been grateful to her grandmother. But she often felt overwhelmed by the woman's strong opinions. So when the opportunity arose to leave home at eighteen, via a marriage that her grandmother had severely questioned, Edith leaped at the chance. Of course, her grandmother thought it was a huge mistake, that Charles was too old for her and that Edith should finish college before marrying. And most disturbing to her grandmother was that Charles wanted to relocate them to Christmas Valley. "A foolish move that you'll one day regret," her grandmother had warned her.

But Edith had never regretted it. Oh, she regretted that the gulf between her and her grandparents had grown wider with each passing year. But with the birth of her first child and the other three so shortly thereafter, she was so distracted with motherhood, her husband's ministry, and all the daily demands of life that contact with her grandparents steadily decreased until it was little more than Christmas and birthday cards.

And then after her children became adults and left home, Edith opened up the bed and breakfast, and her life was just as busy as ever. Her grandfather had died about ten years ago, and her grandmother died the following year. Naturally, she had been saddened to lose them, but then they'd both been in their nineties, so it hadn't been a great surprise. Of course, she did regret that they'd never come out to visit. Even when she specifically invited them to come stay at the newly remodeled B and B, they had declined on account of "health" issues. But she suspected it was merely an excuse.

Myrtle was gathering up the remnants of dough now, slapping them together into a small ball that she proceeded to roll out, back and forth, as if she had done this many a time in the past. Edith no longer cared that Myrtle had taken over. Mostly she felt an overwhelming sense of sadness. She wasn't even sure why.

"You seem to have everything under control here," she told Myrtle as she removed her apron and hung it on the hook by the back door. "Do you mind taking the cookies out of the oven when they're done?"

"Not at all." Myrtle didn't even look up. "Go ahead and do what you need to do. I can handle this by myself. Besides, I'm sure you have a lot to get done before the other guests get here."

"Yes . . ." Edith nodded. But as she walked out of the kitchen, she couldn't think of a single thing that needed doing. Oh, certainly there was plenty to do, but it was as if her usual well-organized mind had been wiped completely clean.

She went up to the room that she and Charles shared. They had remodeled this space for themselves before transforming their home into the Shepherd's Inn. By combining two smaller bedrooms and a bath, they had created a large and comfortable suite that provided a tranquil getaway, a private retreat. And since Charles was visiting a parishioner who was in the hospital in a nearby town, the orderly room was quiet and peaceful now. Edith went inside and closed the door behind her. Then, sitting down in her padded rocking chair, she began to cry. Tears from long ago poured down her cheeks, and she let them. She wasn't quite sure what she was specifically crying for— oh, it had to do with her grandparents, of course, her childhood, their passing . . . but it was all rather vague. Perhaps she was simply grieving.

She wasn't sure just how long she actually cried, but after she'd blown her nose and splashed cold water on her face, it was nearly two o'clock. And she knew it was only a matter of time until the new guests would begin arriving. She *must* pull herself together.

The house was quiet when Edith went back downstairs. She figured that Myrtle was over at the church either helping or harassing Olive. But at least it gave Edith a chance to regroup and get a few things done. To her relief, the cookies looked okay. Perhaps a bit thinner than she would've made them, but at least they hadn't burned. She picked up a lopsided star and took a bite. To be perfectly honest, the anise did make them taste more interesting. She wished there was time to brew a pot of tea, but Edith figured she'd better get busy before the guests started coming. She still needed to put fresh linens in the Good Shepherd Room, where she planned to put Albert Benson, since he was alone and the room was a bit smaller than the others. She also wanted to put the special Christmas mints on the pillows. She'd just picked them up at the Candy Cane Shoppe yesterday afternoon.

"You're going to have your hands full with your new guest," Betty Gordon had told her in a conspirator's tone. Betty was the owner of the candy shop as well as a member of their congregation.

"So you heard her this morning?" ventured Edith.

Betty laughed. "I can imagine she'll really spice things up at the inn."

Edith nodded without commenting.

"Between you and me, I heard that she made a similar scene at Mrs. Santa's Diner."

"Oh, dear . . ."

Betty slipped the package of specialty mints into a red-and-white-striped bag. "It's not my place to say this, but the less time that woman spends in town, the better it will be for everyone, Edith."

"Well, she's helping Olive with the Christmas pageant," said Edith as she put her change into her purse. "That should keep her busy."

"Poor Olive."

Edith nodded. She had been tempted to apologize, but then it wasn't really her fault if a guest behaved badly. Was it?

Edith placed the final mint on the pillow in the Cool Water Room. This room was one of her favorites. All in shades of blue, it was so soothing and peaceful. This was where she planned to put the Thomases. Something the wife had said suggested in her e-mail that the couple had been under a lot of stress lately. Hopefully, this would help.

Edith was just going down the stairs when she heard voices below.

"Hello," she called as she spied a couple standing in the foyer. They looked to be about her age, or maybe younger. "You must be the Fieldses," she said as she shook their hands and introduced herself.

"I'm Carmen," said the woman, then with a slight frown, "and this is Jim."

Jim didn't look too happy.

"We would've been here sooner, but Jim got lost. I begged him to stop and ask directions . . . but you know how men can be."

Edith smiled. "Christmas Valley is a bit off the beaten path."

Then she gave them a brief tour, explained how things worked, gave them some brochures from town, and finally showed them to their room.

"Staff and Rod?" questioned Jim.

"All the rooms are named after portions of the twenty-third psalm," she explained quickly. But still they didn't seem to get it.

"Because this is the Shepherd Inn," she

continued. "And the shepherd uses a staff and rod to keep his sheep safe."

"It sounds more like something he'd use to beat them with," said Carmen.

Edith laughed. "No, no," she said. "A good shepherd would never do that."

She was only a couple steps away when she heard the couple starting to argue. She couldn't discern the words, but she could hear the anger in their voices. Surely they would resolve their differences over their trip and start enjoying their visit before long. At least she hoped so.

Edith was just cleaning up the cookie-making mess when Myrtle came into the kitchen. Tempted to point at the sign above the door, Edith decided it was useless. This woman, not unlike her grandmother, would do just as she pleased.

"I thought I'd find you in here," said Myrtle. "I'm just going to town to get something to eat."

Edith nodded. "That's nice."

"Yes, I thought I should let someone know just in case I have a heart attack on the way." Myrtle frowned.

"Are you feeling unwell?" inquired Edith with a bit of concern.

"No, but it is a bit of a walk, and I'm not as young as I used to be."

Just then Charles came in through the back door. Edith knew he was surprised to see Myrtle in the kitchen, but you couldn't tell by his expression. Of course, this was a trick he'd learned after all his years of pastoring.

"Hello, Myrtle," he said pleasantly. "How are you today?"

She scowled. "I was just telling Edith that having to walk to town for meals is inconvenient for someone like me."

"Can I offer you a ride?" he said with a smile.

She brightened. "Well, now, that'd be just fine."

"Can I pick up anything for you while I'm out?" he asked Edith.

So she gave him a short list, then thanked him. Of course, she was thanking him for transporting Myrtle and getting her out of the inn for a bit.

They had barely left before another guest arrived. This time it was Albert Benson, an elderly man who said very little. Edith tried to be friendly as she guided him to his room, but he kept the conversation short and curt.

Edith couldn't help but feel dismayed as

she went back downstairs. So far her Christmas guests consisted of a cantankerous old woman, a couple who didn't seem to get along too well, and now a moody old man. Oh, she knew that these were probably people who just needed to be loved. But she had so hoped that Christmas would be fun and fulfilling for everyone, and now she was worried that it was going to be stressful and difficult at best.

So Edith did what she usually did whenever she felt worried about something. She sat down at her little desk, bowed her head, and prayed. She asked God to help her and Charles to help each one of her guests, specifically laying their problems out in the same way that she might arrange bath linens, and finally she imagined herself putting all this into God's capable hands as she said "amen."

Then Edith arranged a tempting selection of breads, cookies, and goodies on the dining room table. She also made fresh pots of tea and coffee, then turned on the Christmas music and watered the tall evergreen tree that stood in the corner of the living room. She paused for a moment to savor the comforting ambience of Christmas—the sights and sounds and smells. Yes, she told herself, this Christmas would indeed be different, but it would also be good. And perhaps next year her children would be gathered around her again.

7

By Tuesday afternoon, the Shepherd's Inn was full. Lauren and Michael Thomas, a pleasant thirtysomething couple from Seattle, had arrived just past noon and were settled nicely into the Cool Water Room. And Leslie, the young and recently divorced mother, and her adorable daughter, Megan, had shown up in time for tea.

"Ooh," said Megan with wide eyes when she gazed up at the twelve-foot tree. "Look how big it is, Mommy!"

"This is beautiful," said Leslie as she looked at the various Christmas decorations and admired the setup for afternoon tea. "Much nicer than I expected."

Edith had to admit to herself that it was a great relief to have some guests who truly seemed to appreciate the inn's humble offerings. Perhaps the week wouldn't be so bad after all.

"Would you like to get situated in your room?" suggested Edith. "Then come back down for tea."

"That sounds great," said Leslie as she removed her thick down coat and hung it over her arm. "You know, the forecast said there was no chance of snow, but it's getting so cold outside that I'm not so sure now."

"Snow!" exclaimed Megan, looking at Edith hopefully. "Do you think it could snow in time for Christmas?"

Edith laughed. "Well, you just never know. And it wouldn't be the first time the weatherman was wrong."

As they walked through the foyer, Megan stopped to look at a delicate porcelain sculpture that was situated on a side table, something Edith had had for years. "Ooh, Mommy, look," she said, tugging on her mother's arm. *"An angel."* She reached for it.

"Don't touch, Megan." Leslie gently pulled her back. "It looks very breakable."

"It's managed to survive all my grandchildren so far," said Edith as she escorted them upstairs. She smiled to herself as she opened the door to their room, the Lamb's Room, pausing long enough to hear Megan exclaiming over the small collection of pictures and statues that depicted lambs throughout the room. Clearly, the little girl was pleased. Well, that was something! Edith was feeling more and more hopeful.

After going back downstairs, she poured herself a cup of tea and gazed out the front window as she sipped. It was definitely getting colder out, but the sky was still crisp and clear with not a single cloud in sight. Of course, that could all change quickly enough. That's how it was here in the mountains. In fact, according to the town's historians, that's exactly how it happened back when the original trappers got stuck here so long ago. The weather had started out mild and unseasonably warm before it snapped and turned into one of the biggest blizzards in recorded history. Not that Edith cared to see a snowstorm of that proportion this year, but a nice layer of white for little Megan . . . well, that would be lovely.

The phone in the kitchen rang, jarring Edith back to the present. And when she answered it, the male voice on the other end sounded rather angry. "We have a little problem down here at the North Pole Coffee Shop."

"Who is this calling?"

"This is Mayor Drummel, Edith. And you have a rather eccentric guest who is making a bit of a scene down here," he told her. "Seems she has a problem with Santa Claus."

"Oh, dear." Edith took in a quick breath. "That must be Myrtle . . . and I'm guessing you must be playing Santa today?"

"You got that right. Can you please come down here and get this woman, or do I have to call in the police?"

"Of course," said Edith. "I'll be right there."

Lauren and Michael were just coming in to get tea as Edith was leaving. "I'm terribly sorry," she told them, "but I have to run to town to pick up a guest. Do you mind helping yourselves?"

"Not at all," said Lauren. "This looks yummy."

Edith nodded. "Thank you. I should be right back."

As usual during the week preceding Christmas, Mayor Drummel was outfitted in a very authentic-looking Santa suit, and a line of young children were waiting to sit on his lap. However, Santa was not seated, and the children looked rather unhappy.

"She's in the coffee shop," said the mayor when he spotted Edith. "I told her to either go in there and shut up, or risk going to jail."

"I'm so sorry," began Edith.

"Just take her away," demanded the mayor in a hushed voice. "She's ruining everything. Do you know that she actually told the children that I was a fake and that there is no such thing as Santa Claus?"

Edith just shook her head. "I am so terribly sorry."

"Just get her out of here," he said as he turned and headed back to his big velvet-covered chair. "Everything's going to be okay now, children," he said in a big, dramatic Santa-style voice. "*Ho-ho-ho!* That poor old woman was very naughty when she was a little girl, and all I ever put in her stocking was lumps of coal and switches."

The children's eyes grew wide with worry,

as if they too might've been naughty a time or two.

"But don't fret," he told them in a reassuring tone. "You're all good children, and I'm sure that I'll be bringing you something much better."

Edith hurried into the North Pole Coffee Shop, unsure as to what she might find. Perhaps Myrtle would be standing on a chair and telling the customers to repent of all Christmas folly lest they be doomed forever.

Fortunately, that was not the case. Myrtle was quietly sitting at the counter, sipping a cup of coffee.

"I heard there was a problem . . ." Edith spoke in a quiet voice as she took the empty stool next to Myrtle. She was well aware of the eyes that were watching her now. And she felt certain that they wanted her to get the crazy woman out of here, the sooner the better. Still, she didn't want to do anything to rock Myrtle's boat. That would probably just make things worse.

"Wasn't much of a problem," said Myrtle in a matter-of-fact voice. "I just wanted to set the children straight. Grown-ups shouldn't be lying to children."

"It's just for fun," explained Edith.

"Well, I told those kids that they should come to church and see the Christmas pageant if they wanted to know what Christmas was really about."

"You didn't?" Edith was horrified. What a terrible way to invite people to their church! Good grief, Myrtle might as well have been carrying a gun. No wonder Mayor Drummel was so upset. As far as Edith knew, that poor man had never set foot in church in his entire life. And this would probably set him back light-years.

"I did," retorted Myrtle. "And I'd do it again if necessary."

"Please, don't."

"Well, it's a shame letting children think that Christmas is nothing but Santa Claus and ho-ho-ho. Someone should tell them the truth."

"In due time, Myrtle," said Edith. "I'm sure the children will all hear the truth in due time."

Finally, Myrtle was done with her coffee, and Edith quietly escorted her out a side door and to her car that was parked in back.

"It's cold out here," said Myrtle as she climbed in the car. "I can feel snow in my old bones."

"I hope so," said Edith, thankful to change the subject from Santa to snow. "We've got a sweet little girl at the inn who is praying for snow." She looked up toward the mountains and noticed a thick layer of clouds that was accumulating there.

"*Praying* for snow?" Myrtle shook her head in obvious disapproval as she made a *tsk-tsk* sound.

Edith decided not to engage. "All the guests have arrived now. The inn is full."

"No room at the inn, eh?"

Edith smiled. "Yes, I guess you could say that." Of course, she was also thinking that it would be nice if a certain room, a room that was occupied by a certain cantankerous woman, would suddenly vacate. However, she could never admit such an ungracious thing to a single soul. Besides, she reminded herself, this Christmas was about being hospitable to strangers. And she'd certainly never had a guest who was any stranger than Myrtle Pinkerton!

All the guests, except Albert Benson, were having tea in the dining room when Edith and Myrtle walked in. It was nice to see they'd introduced themselves and were now comfortably chatting with each other. To her relief, Charles had emerged from his study to join them and was currently talking to Jim Fields about Australia. It seemed that the Fieldses had spent their last Christmas down under. And Lauren and Michael were visiting with little Megan, telling her that they too thought it might snow for Christmas. In many ways, it wasn't so unlike one big happy family.

Edith introduced Myrtle to the other guests, hoping that this unpredictable woman wouldn't do something to immediately alienate herself from the rest of the group, but to her surprise, Myrtle seemed in good spirits now. And soon she was visiting with Leslie, examining her knitted vest, and giving her tips on how Leslie could've done it even better. Oh, well.

Edith went to the kitchen to make a fresh pot of tea. As she turned on the teakettle, she wondered about Myrtle and what they would do about her. Perhaps it would be best if they restricted her from going to town at all. Edith could offer to fix her simple meals to eat in the kitchen, since she spent half her time in there anyway. But how could they force her to comply? It wasn't as if they were her legal guardians. Perhaps Charles would have some ideas.

The afternoon tea party slowly broke up, with some people going to town, others to their rooms. Charles joined Edith in the kitchen. "Everything going okay?" he asked, and she suspected that her face, as usual, was giving away her concerns.

So she told him about the little fiasco in town with Myrtle. Of course, this only made him laugh. "I can just imagine the look on poor Drummel's face," he said after he'd recovered.

"That's not all," she continued, telling him how Myrtle had "invited" everyone to the church's Christmas pageant.

He shook his head. "Well, don't worry, Edith, I doubt that it'll make a difference one way or another. And, besides, I'm sure she meant well."

"Just the same, I think we should have a talk with her," said Edith.

"Meaning, *I* should have a talk with her?"

"Well, you're better at these things . . .

"Perhaps we can make it seem as if she's our special guest," said Edith suddenly. "We can tell her that since she doesn't have a car and it's difficult for her to get to town . . . that we'd like her to share meals with us. Would that be okay?"

He nodded. "That sounds like a wise plan."

So they put it to her, and to Edith's great surprise and relief, Myrtle seemed perfectly fine with this idea. When the three of them sat down to a humble meal of black-bean soup and cornbread, Edith looked out the kitchen window. She saw that fluffy white snowflakes, illuminated by the back-porch light, were tumbling down.

"It's snowing," she said with childlike enthusiasm. "Perhaps it'll be a white Christmas after all."

Charles nodded. "The weatherman is wrong again."

"They should hire weathermen with old bones like mine," commented Myrtle. "Then they'd know for sure if it was going to rain or snow. My joints have been aching something fierce all day."

"Well, I'm sure that it didn't help to walk back and forth to town," said Edith. "Fortunately, you won't have to do that anymore."

Myrtle just nodded without commenting, and for some reason Edith wasn't so sure she was going to be able to keep Myrtle from her anti-Christmas antics. She might have to keep a special eye on this woman during the next few days.

It had been a long day, but it finally seemed as if things were settling down at the Shepherd's Inn. The guests were all back from their various dinner places. Even the somber Albert Benson had ventured out. Now everyone was in their rooms, and Edith and Charles were turning off the downstairs lights when they heard a knock at the door.

"Who could that be at this hour?" asked Edith.

"We'll soon find out," said Charles as he went to open the door. A blast of chilly winter air mixed with snow burst in, and there on the porch stood a young couple.

Edith blinked as she looked over Charles's shoulder to see them better. These people looked as if they'd stepped right out of time. The tall, narrow-faced man had long brown hair and a full beard, and the shoulders of his dark woolen coat were dusted with snow. But it was the young woman who got Edith's attention with her sad dark eyes and a cascade of curls beneath a plaid woven scarf that was wrapped around her head.

"Do you have a room for the night?" asked the young man.

Charles looked at Edith, then back at the couple. "I'm sorry, but the inn is full until after Christmas."

The woman sadly nodded. "I told you they'd be full up, Collin," she said.

"Why don't you come in," suggested Charles. "That way we can close the door and keep the heat inside."

So the couple stepped into the foyer and, shaking powdery snow from their clothes, they looked around the inn and seemed impressed.

"This is a real nice place you got," said the man.

"It's so pretty," said the woman.

"Where are you two from?" asked Charles.

"Montana," said the woman. "We're heading to California."

"California?" echoed Edith. "Aren't you a little off course?"

The woman made a half smile. "Well, Collin picked the straightest route going west. Then we planned to head due south to San Diego where his brother lives."

"But we were having some engine troubles," explained Collin.

"And then the weather hit," she added. "It's a real blizzard out there."

"And so we thought we'd treat ourselves to a room for just one night," said Collin. "Just to get cleaned up, you know. But that's okay, we're pretty low on funds anyway, we can stay in our bus."

"Your bus?" queried Charles.

Collin nodded toward the big picture window that looked out over the street. "Yeah, it's all set up to live in with a bed and everything. Not the Ritz or anything. But comfy enough."

Edith went over to peer out onto the street, but all she could see was dark shadows and snow flurries.

"Do you mind if we leave it parked there?" asked the woman. "On the street I mean? Just for the night, you know?"

"Or until I have time to tweak on the engine a little," Collin added. "It's running pretty badly right now."

Charles looked at Edith, and she just shrugged. "I don't see that it's a problem," she said.

"You wouldn't think so," said Charles. "Not for just one night."

"Do you need anything?" asked Edith. "Food or anything?"

The woman's eyes lit up. "We're low on water. And, hey, if you want to share some food . . . that'd be cool. We're pretty broke. Just trying to get down to San Diego so that Collin can find work, you know."

"Come on in the kitchen," said Edith, forgetting her sign again. "We've got some leftovers from dinner that you can have if you like. By the way, my name is Edith, and my husband is Charles."

"Oh, I'm sorry," said the woman. "We didn't even introduce ourselves. I'm Amy and," she jerked her thumb over a shoulder, "that's Collin."

In the brighter light of the kitchen, Edith could see that Amy was quite young. Probably early twenties at the most. And she also appeared to be quite pregnant.

"You're expecting?" said Edith as she put the bean soup into the microwave to heat.

"Yeah. My due date is actually the first week of January. But my back's been aching, and I feel as big as a house right now. I wouldn't mind if it came tonight."

"Tonight?" Edith felt her brows shooting up. "But what would you do? The hospital is nearly an hour away, and that's in good weather."

"Oh, I plan to have it naturally, at home." She laughed. "Or in the bus."

"Really?" Edith wrapped a generous chunk of cornbread in plastic wrap and put this into a grocery sack, along with several pieces of fruit.

"You mind if I fill this up in here?" asked Collin as he appeared with a large water jug.

"That's fine," said Edith. "Or if it's easier, go ahead and use the laundry sink out on the back porch."

Now Charles was in the kitchen too.

"Amy is expecting a baby soon," said Edith in what she hoped sounded like a calm voice.

"Yeah," said Amy. "The sooner the better. Although I suppose it might be easier to have it in San Diego. Not to mention warmer."

"It must be hard on you to travel," said Charles.

"Not really," she said. "If my back starts hurting, I just go lie down on the bed. But the bouncing gets to me sometimes. Do you have any idea how bouncy a bus can be?"

Charles just shook his head.

"Here you go," said Edith as she handed Amy the bag of food. "And you two feel free to come in and get some breakfast in the morning. There'll be plenty to go around."

"Seriously?" Amy looked truly surprised.

"Of course," said Edith. "You're more than welcome."

Now Collin emerged with his full water jug. "You guys are way cool," he said with a bright smile. "I told Amy that there were still a few good people left in this world."

Charles smiled at them. "Well, let's hope so."

They walked the couple to the door and told them good night. "Sleep well," called Edith as they went back out into the snow. She wanted to add "and don't go into labor," but that didn't sound quite right. Still, she really hoped that the baby would wait until the parents had safely made their destination in sunny Southern California.

"Wasn't that something?" said Charles as he locked the door.

"They seemed nice," said Edith. "I wish we had an available room. I'd let them have it for free."

He put his arm around her shoulder. "I know you would, dear. That's just one of the many things I love about you."

And then they went up to bed.

8

"What on earth is *that*?" exclaimed Myrtle when she came into Edith's kitchen.

"What?" Edith looked up from her daily devotions, trying not to seem as aggravated as she felt. Myrtle was such an early riser that Edith would have to start getting up a lot earlier if she expected to have a decent quiet time these days. As it was, she was already tiptoeing downstairs long before daylight.

"That hideous contraption that's parked in front of your inn is what."

Edith went to the living room and looked out the big picture window in front. "Oh, my . . ." Her hand flew up to her mouth as she remembered their late-night visitors. "That's, uh, very interesting."

"It's atrocious!"

"Well, it's certainly colorful." Edith smiled to herself as she studied the wild-colored stripes and flowers and geometric designs. "It looks like a hippie bus—straight out of the sixties."

"I'll say," said Myrtle with a look of disgust. "How in the world do you think it got here?"

So Edith explained about the young couple's unexpected arrival the night before. "We told them it was okay to park there for the night." She chuckled. "But we hadn't actually seen their bus since it was dark out."

"Well, you sure can't miss it now."

Even with the thick white cap of snow on top, you couldn't miss the brightly colored bus. In fact, the clean blanket of snow all around only made the bus stand out more. "Well, don't worry," said Edith. "They'll probably be gone by noon." Then she returned to the kitchen, dismayed to see that Myrtle was right on her heels. "They're just a couple of young people, on their way to California, hopefully in time for the baby."

"Baby?" Myrtle frowned. "You mean people are traveling in that old dilapidated thing and they're about to have a baby? That sounds plum crazy to me." She lowered her voice. "Do you think they're drug people?"

Edith sighed. "I don't think so."

"Well, I remember when the kids who lived in vehicles like that were all a bunch of druggies. A bunch of social outcasts who wanted to turn on or drop out or something to that effect. Horrible way to raise a baby, if you ask me."

Edith wanted to remind Myrtle that no one had asked her, but instead she asked her to stir the pancake batter.

Breakfast came and went without an appearance of the mysterious young couple who inhabited the colorful bus on the street. At first Edith felt relieved, as it alleviated the need to explain exactly who these people were to her paying guests. But then, as she was clearing the table and cleaning up, she began to feel some strong twinges of guilt. What if something was wrong? What if they had frozen to death out there? Or what if they'd had a gas leak and were asphyxiated? Or what if Amy had gone into labor and needed medical help?

Finally, Edith was so distraught that she couldn't concentrate on rinsing the plates, so she pulled on her fleece-lined snow boots and her heavy coat and hurried outside to check on them. Oh, certainly, she felt a bit intrusive as she knocked on the door, but really, what if something was seriously wrong? How could she not check?

After she knocked loudly several times and called out their names, a sleepy-looking Collin appeared at the window and opened the door. He was shirtless and blinking, almost as if he wasn't sure where he was. "Yeah?" he said in a gruff voice. "Something wrong?"

"No, I, uh," Edith stammered, "I—uh—I was just worried that something might be wrong out here. Were you warm enough?"

He nodded, realization coming to his face. "Yeah, no problem. It's pretty cozy in here. You don't need to worry."

"Well, come on into the inn if you want breakfast," she told him. "I've put aside some things for you and Amy."

"Sure, thanks." He smiled and closed the door.

Edith felt a bit silly and neurotic as she hurried back into the inn. Of course, they were perfectly fine. Why wouldn't they be? Probably just tired from their long journey yesterday. And she had forgotten that all young people seemed to enjoy sleeping in. Certainly her own children had been late risers. Still, that bit that Myrtle had tossed in about possible drug use did raise a smidgen of doubt in her mind. But, surely, a pregnant mother would have better sense than that. Wouldn't she?

It was nearly eleven when Collin and Amy came in for breakfast, but Edith tried to appear as if this were perfectly normal. She even poured herself a cup of tea and sat down with them, attempting to make light conversation.

"Do you know what's wrong with your engine?" she finally asked, hoping that it didn't sound too rude, as if she were hinting that these two should be on their way.

"Not exactly," said Collin. "I'm not real mechanical, if you know what I mean."

"Charles knows a bit about engines," she said absently.

"Do you suppose he could take a look?" asked Amy hopefully.

"Oh, I forgot this is Wednesday," Edith said. "Not a very good day for Charles to help."

"What does he do on Wednesdays?" asked Collin.

"He's a pastor," she told them. "The church across the street. He usually does the final revision of his midweek service on Wednesdays."

"Oh." Amy sighed and rubbed her large belly.

Seeing their disappointment, Edith quickly said, "But I can certainly ask him if he has some spare time." Also, she realized, if someone didn't get that engine running, the strange-looking bus wouldn't be going anywhere.

After the young couple finished their breakfast, Edith went and tapped on the door to Charles's study. "Sorry to disturb you," she began, then launched into the need for someone with mechanical expertise to help with the bus.

He set down his pen and closed his Bible. "That's quite a bus."

She made a half smile. "Anyway, I thought about calling Hal Berry," she continued, "but I wasn't sure that was such a good idea. I know his arthritis has been acting up lately."

Charles smiled. "I'll take a look at it, Edith.

I think my sermon is in good shape, and I'm happy to lend a hand—if I can, that is."

"And it might help to get them on their way. You know, before anyone from town starts to make a fuss. I have to admit that their bus really does look a bit out of place out there."

Just then the phone rang, and Charles answered it. "It's Polly, Edith," he told her. "Want to take it in here while I go see what can be done?"

So Edith sank down into his big leather chair and said, "Hello, Polly."

"What is going on over at the inn?" asked Polly.

Edith laughed. "You mean our hippie bus?"

"Yes. Herb told me about it this morning. He'd seen it on his way into town when he got gas for our trip. But it sounded so outrageous that I actually thought he was making it up. As we were leaving town a bit ago, I made him drive by just so I could see it for myself. I'm calling you on my cell phone. Now I can't stand to leave town without knowing what's up over there."

So Edith explained about the young couple, even the part about the soon-to-be-born baby.

"Good grief!" said Polly. "I wish I could stick around and see what happens next. First it's that crazy Myrtle who seems determined to convert Christmas Valley to something—I don't even know what. And then it's a hippie bus straight out of the blue. Why, the next thing we know, you'll probably be out there helping to deliver a baby on Christmas day."

"Goodness, I hope not. I've never been very good in that situation. I had to be practically knocked out to deliver my own children. If Amy needed help, I suppose I could call up Helen—that's assuming she can remember anything about nursing since she's been retired for years."

"That'd be something else with Helen's bad knees and fading eyesight. I can just see it. Well, keep me informed, Edith. If it gets any more interesting, that is."

"Travel safely," said Edith. "The roads looked pretty slick this morning."

"Right. And have a merry Christmas, Edith. You and all your crazy guests and those hippie bus people too." Then she laughed and hung up.

Edith set the phone down. She supposed they must look a bit crazy to anyone from the outside looking in. But, really, Collin and Amy seemed like nice people, just a little down on their luck perhaps. Even Myrtle in her own way wasn't so bad. Sure, perhaps a bit eccentric and even obnoxious at times, but underneath that Edith thought she had a good heart.

"Leave me alone!" she heard a man's voice yelling and then the loud banging of a door. It seemed to be coming from the second floor, so Edith jumped up and dashed up the stairs to see.

"What's wrong?" she breathlessly asked Myrtle when she saw her standing in front of the Good Shepherd Room, the room where old Albert Benson was staying. "What happened?"

Myrtle shrugged with big innocent eyes. "I don't know."

"But I heard yelling up here," she continued. "Was it Mr. Benson? Is he okay? What's wrong?"

"He's a very moody man," said Myrtle as she turned and headed back toward her room on the other side of the hallway.

Just then Mr. Benson opened the door

and stuck his head out. "I'm not moody," he said in a defensive voice. "I just don't wish to be bothered."

"Then why did you come here?" demanded Myrtle. "Why come to a bed and breakfast?"

Edith blinked. "Perhaps it was for some peace and quiet," she said. And normally that would be exactly what her guests could expect to find.

"During Christmas?" Myrtle looked skeptical.

"It's none of your business," he retorted. Edith hoped that was meant for Myrtle.

"That's right," Edith said in a soothing voice. "It's not our business. I just wanted to make sure you were okay, Mr. Benson."

"I'll be perfectly fine as long as *that woman* leaves me alone."

"Did you hear him, Myrtle?" asked Edith, suddenly feeling as if she had gone about twenty years back in time and was now talking to her own bickering children. "Mr. Benson would like you to leave him alone."

Myrtle shrugged again. "That's what he says . . . but if he wanted to be left alone, he should've just stayed home."

And at that, Mr. Benson slammed his door shut again.

Edith couldn't help but roll her eyes. "Please, Myrtle," she said, struggling to keep her voice calm and even. "Leave the poor man alone. I'm begging you."

"Fine," said Myrtle. "But you'll be sorry."

"*I'll* be sorry?"

Myrtle nodded without saying anything, then scuffled off to her room.

Edith sighed and walked away. More and more she was wondering whether she was running an inn or a nuthouse.

Hopefully, they'd all make it through Christmas without killing each other. She had to chuckle as she went down the stairs. In some ways this was a lot more like having her family there than she'd ever imagined possible. Suddenly she remembered how Katie and Krista usually got into at least one little, or sometimes big, snit before the holidays were over. Or how Tommy and Jack could get so competitive that they would bore everyone to tears by trying to one-up each other in their accomplishments. Well, what families always got along perfectly, anyway? Just as long as no one got hurt.

"I'm afraid that bus is in no condition to travel," announced Charles as he came into the kitchen and washed his hands in the sink. "Not without some serious mechanical work, not to mention expense."

"Do they have any money to fix it?"

"Not to speak of . . . and we, I mean the church, could probably help them. But I'd have to call an emergency board meeting first . . . and it's not the best time of year for that . . . I'm not sure . . ." He shook his head. "Besides the engine, the tires are bald, and they don't even have chains to get over the mountain pass. Kids these days."

"Well, you know what the Good Book says . . ." Edith smiled.

"I do and I don't. What do you mean?"

"That God watches out for fools and children."

He nodded. "Well, I think they could fit into both categories." He scratched his head. "Collin told me that Amy is only nineteen. *Nineteen?* Can you believe it? I mean, our baby Krista is seven years older than that, and I couldn't imagine her in this position."

"Well, she would never put herself in this position, dear."

"And Collin is only twenty-one. They really aren't much more than children, Edith."

"Yes. But don't forget that I was even younger when we got married, Charles. And not even twenty-one when we had Tommy."

"But you were mature," he argued. "You were old for your age."

She laughed. "Thanks. I guess."

He sighed. "I just don't know what to do about them."

"Well, it's not as if you have to figure it all out today," she said. "Besides, if they spend another night, they might come to church tonight. And that might be a good thing for them, don't you think?"

He smiled now. "Perhaps you're right, my dear. Perhaps it would."

And as it turned out, Edith was right. Not only were they willing, but the young couple was happy to come to church with her.

"We're only going because of you guys," said Amy after Edith invited the two of them to come. "You and your husband have been so kind that it's making us rethink some of our opinions about church and religion and stuff."

It was after seven when Edith walked across the freshly plowed street to the church. She knew she was running late, but there'd been so many distractions at the inn this afternoon. Mainly because of Myrtle. It seemed that woman had gotten some kind of a bee in her bonnet about poor Albert Benson. But Edith wasn't sure what her real motives were—was she flirting with the old man or just trying to drive him batty? Edith finally had to plead with Charles to step in and intervene. Fortunately, Mr. Benson seemed to appreciate this, and he didn't even mind heading over to the church thirty minutes early so that he could help Charles with a stubborn lock, since they'd just learned that Mr. Benson was a retired locksmith.

Of course, this left Myrtle at loose ends again, and as a result she had started offering "marriage counseling" tips to the Fieldses. Not that they didn't need some help in that regard, for it was plain to see that this couple had some real issues. But Myrtle hardly seemed the answer. Finally Edith persuaded Myrtle to head over to church herself, and after the meddling old woman was gone, Edith tried to smooth things over with the feuding Fieldses.

"Myrtle's one of those people who likes to have her finger in every pie," offered Edith. "I hope you won't take her words too seriously."

Carmen Fields, sitting on the sofa with

arms crossed tightly across her front, still looked upset. "Well, she made a good point. Jim *does* seem to take me for granted."

"Who takes *who* for granted?" he shot back at her.

"You do!" snapped Carmen. "We've been married almost thirty years, and I'll bet I can count on one hand how many times you've told me that you appreciate me."

"That's not true!"

And on they went until the rest of the guests quietly slipped away, either to church or to the Christmas play that the town was putting on tonight. Finally, Edith excused herself too. And consequently, she was late to church.

9

When she got to church, Edith wasn't terribly surprised to see that Myrtle was, once again, in her seat. And since she was late, Edith decided to sit in the back. Sure it felt strange, but in light of everything else it seemed fitting. It was as if her world were getting turned upside down, or perhaps tilting sideways. Hopefully, things would improve by Christmas. The idea of having a houseful of bickering guests over the holidays made Edith want to run away from home.

She scanned the backs of heads, recognizing old friends and neighbors as well as a few of their guests. She was just late enough to have missed introductions, and she desperately hoped that Myrtle hadn't done anything to upset anyone's applecart, specifically Mr. Benson's. But all seemed calm and normal. And the church was fuller than usual, although that still meant that more than half the seats were vacant.

She noticed Collin and Amy, only a couple of rows ahead of her, and she might have imagined it, but it seemed that when Charles came to the challenging part of his sermon, Collin leaned forward just a bit as if trying to soak the words in. That was encouraging. Perhaps the delay of their departure really was for a good reason. Maybe these two young people would take away something good—perhaps even something life changing—before they left Christmas Valley for good.

Just three days until Christmas Eve, she told herself as the service wound down and they stood to sing the anthem. *So much to be done.* And, she wondered, was it really worth all the work and effort? Oh, it was one thing to stretch herself this thin for her own family and loved ones, but what had she been thinking to go to this much trouble for a bunch of strangers? Somewhat cantankerous strangers at that. Just then some of the words from Charles's sermon last week drifted through her mind. *Showing hospitality to strangers . . . perhaps entertaining angels unaware . . .*

She looked again at the young couple standing just ahead of her. Collin had his arm draped protectively over Amy's shoulders as he gave her a little squeeze. So seemingly vulnerable and in such a desperate state of need, and to think these two were about to become parents! It must be overwhelming. Would these young people be able to make it? Goodness knows they barely had a roof over their heads.

And that's when something hit her— almost as if God himself had whacked her over the head with a hymnal. She actually jumped. Why hadn't she considered this before? This struggling young couple wasn't so different from sweet Mary and Joseph so long ago! And, not unlike Jesus's parents, Collin and Amy had found no room at the inn as well! How interestingly ironic! In fact, here she'd been thinking about hospitality and angels and, well . . . but the song ended, and she was quickly brought back to the here and now by her husband's voice. He was making an announcement.

"There will be an unscheduled board meeting tonight," Charles was telling the congregation. "We'll meet in the conference room, and it, hopefully, won't take too long."

Edith assumed this must be the "emergency meeting" he'd mentioned earlier. He was probably going to try to convince the board to help this young couple. Feeling reassured, she smiled brightly at her husband. He was such a good man. And then the church began to empty to the soft tones of Marie's organ playing.

"What is going on at the inn?" demanded Olive before Edith even had a chance to slip into her coat.

Edith blinked. "What do you mean?"

"That bus."

"Oh, that . . ." Edith forced a smile. "It's temporarily stranded, Olive. But I think you'll hear more about that at the board meeting tonight."

"Well, hopefully, it won't be there for long. It looks perfectly terrible, Edith. And don't you forget that the pageant is only two nights away. It had better be gone by then, or I'll want to know the reason why."

Now Helen limped over to join them. She was using a shiny black cane to help her walk. Edith hoped that Helen didn't have any lawsuit plans in mind—that would surely send the church insurance sky-high. "Are you talking about that monstrosity out in front of the inn?" she asked.

Edith glanced over to the aisle to see if Collin and Amy were close enough to over-hear any of this. Fortunately, it looked like they weren't. But it also looked as if no one in the entire congregation was speaking to them either. Edith longed to go over and join them, make them feel welcome, but she was completely blocked in her pew by Olive and Helen as they discussed the inappropriate-ness of the colorful bus parked across the street.

"Not only that," continued Helen, now turning her attention to Edith, "but Clarence said that Mayor Drummel plans to give you a call. He's not the least bit happy with this. Es-pecially at Christmas."

"Oh . . ." Edith was distracted by the

young couple. They were slipping out the front door mostly unnoticed, probably going back to their bus, which was likely cold. She was just about to rush over and stop them. She didn't know what she'd say or do, but somehow she had to—

"Did you hear me?" demanded Helen. "The mayor is going to call you on this, Edith Ryan. Aren't you the least bit concerned?"

Edith watched the door close behind the couple, then looked at her watch in dismay. "Are you ladies planning to attend the board meeting?" she asked suddenly.

"That's right," said Olive crisply as she took Helen by the arm that wasn't attached to the cane. "Let's go."

Now, although Edith, being the pastor's wife, was welcome to sit in on board meetings, she rarely did. She found the conversations not only dull, but usually rather frustrating. It seemed that some people, particularly board member types, liked hearing the sounds of their own voices more than they did resolving issues. And often they would end up in a big argument, and the meeting would adjourn, and everyone would go home disgruntled. Then they would talk among themselves during the week, some holding a grudge, others just hurt. Finally, they would meet again, and worn out from the battle, they would work out some sort of compromise. She hoped that wouldn't be the case tonight, since the plight of Collin and Amy seemed rather urgent.

And so she decided that perhaps this was a good night for her to sit in. With people like Olive and Helen already so worked up about the presence of the bus, who knew what might happen tonight. The board members might emerge from the church with torches, storm across the street, and beat on the bus as they demanded that the "hippies leave town!" Oh, she knew she was being overly dramatic, but at the same time she might not be too far off either. So, filled with trepidation, she headed for the conference room, and hoping to be inconspicuous, she took a seat by the door.

In his usual formal way, Hal Berry called the meeting to order. "As you know, this is an emergency board meeting," he said, "requested by Pastor Charles, and being that it's the holidays, our good pastor has promised to keep it short."

Then Charles stood up. "I'm sure you've all seen the bus across the street. . . ."

Several sarcastic twitters and indistin-
guishable comments assured Edith that
she'd been right to come. And as her husband made his plea, she could tell by their
expressions that most of the board members
were not feeling sympathetic to Charles's
straightforward request for assistance.

"Why should we help *them*?" asked Olive
after he sat down. "They don't even live
here."

"That's right," added Helen. "If we're going
to help someone, why not start in our own
town. We have young families who are struggling to make ends meet right here in Christmas Valley, and they're just as needy as
those—those *bus people*."

"I don't know about that," said Peter Simpson, the youngest member of the board. "We
don't have anyone in town who's actually living in a bus."

"And who lives in a bus?" demanded
Olive. "For all we know, these people could
be drug dealers. They do have that sort of
look about them."

"Maybe we should let the law intervene,"
suggested Hal. "They might be better suited
to handle something like this."

And on they went, back and forth and getting nowhere fast. As was her custom, Edith just sat and listened, until finally she did something she'd never done before. "May I say something?" she asked.

The room got quiet, and everyone looked at her.

"I know I'm not an official member of the board, but I really would like to say something."

"Go right ahead, Edith," said Hal in a kind voice. Charles smiled at her.

She stood up, feeling slightly light-headed and more than a little self-conscious, unsure if she could even continue. Speaking in front of a group, even one as small as this, had never been her strong suit. She hoped she was really up to the task. "I understand your concerns about our, uh, our *visitors*. And I realize their accommodations are a bit, well, shall I say unconventional?" More twitters. "But as I was sitting in church tonight, I was remembering what Charles had preached on just last week . . . about showing kindness and hospitality to strangers . . . and how sometimes we might be actually entertaining angels or our Lord without even knowing it. And as I was looking at this young couple, Collin and Amy, it occurred to me that they are in very similar straits as another couple . . . it occurred to me that more than two thousand years ago, Mary and Joseph were strangers in town too. They were looking for a place to stay . . . and, well, I just thought perhaps this is the Lord's doing. Perhaps he has sent Collin and Amy to remind us of something. Or maybe it's simply our opportunity to show kindness and hospitality. Or . . ." She lowered her voice now, almost afraid to actually put to words what was really on her mind. "Or is it possible that they might be angels or even our Lord himself in disguise? How could we ever know this for sure? But even if that's not the case, don't you think that our Lord would want us to open our hearts to them? To welcome them as if they were sent down from heaven above?"

Now the room got very silent for a long moment, and Edith, with nothing more to say, was almost afraid to breathe.

"Oh, that's ridiculous," said Olive finally. "They're obviously *not* angels."

"Of course not," agreed Helen. "And the Lord?" She shook her head.

"Arriving in that hideous bus?" added Olive.

"And yet," said Helen, with a thoughtful expression across her brow, "and yet . . . I think I am starting to see Edith's point."

And just like that, the attitude in the room began to shift and transform until not only was the board willing to pay for all the mechanical expenses *and* new tires, but Helen was talking about giving an impromptu baby shower for Amy.

"But they'll be leaving soon," protested Olive. "There'll be no reason for them to stick around once their bus is running."

"Then we'll have to jump right on it," said Helen with excitement. "I'll bet you that they don't have a single thing for that baby. Do they, Edith?"

Edith held up her hands. "I really don't know. But I guess I could find out."

"Right," said Helen. "You find out and call me first thing in the morning. Don't worry, I'll take care of the rest."

Edith's heart and heels were happy as she and Charles walked across the street later on that night. "It's just so amazing," she told him. "I don't ever remember the board being so generous, so quickly, before."

He squeezed her hand. "Well, you made a

beautiful plea, dear. I don't know how they could've turned their backs after what you said."

"Do you think it sounded crazy?" she ventured. "I mean the part about them possibly being angels or even our Lord? Goodness, I don't want everyone to think that I'm losing my marbles."

"No, I think it sounded very tenderhearted and compassionate. And who knows? Maybe they are angels unaware."

Snowflakes were starting to fall again as Edith paused on the sidewalk to look over to where the bus was parked. For a few seconds she just stared and wondered. Wouldn't it be like God to send angels in a funny old vehicle like that—so quirky and unexpected? So unlike anything that humans would think of doing. But hadn't it been like that when the Lord Jesus was born in a humble barn? And as she went to sleep that night, she felt a deep and comforting sense of peace, as if she really was on the right track after all.

The next morning, Edith was happily puttering in her kitchen, getting cinnamon rolls into the oven and just starting up a pot of coffee, when the phone rang. "Shepherd's Inn," she sang out cheerfully.

"Edith Ryan?" said a male voice.

"Yes?"

"This is Mayor Drummel. I'm sorry to call so early, but I hadn't really planned to be in my office today, and I wanted to take care of this as soon as possible." He cleared his throat. "There's been concern expressed over the rather outlandish vehicle that's been parked in front of your inn."

"Yes?" Edith didn't know what to say.

"Well, I wanted to let you know that they'll need to leave as soon as possible. City ordinances do not allow for this type of vehicle to be parked in town. This morning won't be a bit too soon."

"But that might not be possible, Mayor Drummel. You see, they're broken down, and although our church is going to help them with mechanics and whatnot, I seriously doubt that the bus will be up and running anytime this morning."

"So they are leaving, then?"

"Of course. I'm sure they'll leave as soon as it's possible."

"Because it doesn't look good, Edith. I

mean, we're a town that prides ourselves on appearances, especially at Christmastime. I'm sure you must understand the importance of this since you run a very nice inn and Charles oversees the town's only church—a rundown old bus that's broken down in the street doesn't reflect well on you folks either. If necessary, we could probably have them towed away."

Now, this rubbed Edith wrong. And while she didn't care to take the mayor to task, she thought perhaps a gentle reminder might be in order. "I can respect your concern," she began, "but you must remember that these are *real* people with *real* problems, and you can't simply brush them away as if they were garbage—especially at Christmas. If we're a town that really cares about Christmas, I'd think that we'd all want to reach out in the spirit of charity and help them out."

The mayor didn't respond to this.

"We'll do whatever we can to get their vehicle up and running," said Edith in a firm voice. "I just can't make any promises as to how soon that will be."

"But what about your church's pageant tomorrow night?"

"A bus on the street will hardly stop a Christmas pageant."

"But it won't look good, Edith."

Edith was looking out the window now, staring at the brightly painted bus, which suddenly reminded her of a giant Christmas ornament. "Beauty is in the eyes of the beholder," she said simply enough.

"*What?* What do you mean by that?"

"I mean that we are a town that loves to celebrate Christmas, and this year it seems that we are also the lucky recipients of a *Christmas bus*, and I happen to think it's rather beautiful."

"Oh."

After telling the mayor "Good day," Edith put on her coat and boots and hurried outside to check on Amy and Collin. She was surprised to see that about four more inches of snow had fallen during the night, bringing the accumulation to the top of her boots. Edith trudged through the snow and then knocked on the bus's door. This time Amy answered, but it looked as if they were already awake and dressed. Collin was sitting in the driver's seat, hunched over as he studied a worn map with a rather dismal expression.

"Sorry to bother you," Edith began.

"No bother." Amy held the door open. "Want to come in?"

Edith hesitated, then quickly said, "Yes, that'd be nice."

The interior of the bus was crowded with all manner of boxes and bags and, Edith's nose suspected, a fair amount of dirty laundry too. But Amy cleared a spot on a wooden crate and pointed for Edith to sit down. "It's not much," Amy apologized. "But, hey, it's better than nothing."

Edith nodded, glancing to the back of the bus where a mattress, heaped with quilts and blankets, was wedged. "It is cozy."

"You can say that again," said Amy. "And the bigger I get with this baby, the cozier it seems to get. I can't wait to get out of here. Collin's going to get work when we get settled, and then we'll rent something. Even a one-bedroom apartment will feel like a mansion compared to this."

"Speaking of the baby," began Edith, "I, uh, *we* were wondering if you have everything you need for it."

Amy shrugged. "I have a few things. Like some sleepers and blankets that I got at Salvation Army back home. And Collin got some newborn-sized disposable diapers that are in here . . ." She looked around. "Somewhere."

Edith nodded. "Yes, and that's a good start. But some of the women at church got this idea last night . . . they thought it would be fun to have a baby shower—"

"A baby shower!" Amy's eyes lit up. "Oh, man, I've been wishing for a baby shower. But we didn't really have anyone who wanted to do it. I mean, my family is, well, you know, a little dysfunctional. And Collin's family, well, they live all over the country."

Edith could feel Collin watching her now, and she wasn't sure what he was thinking, but she turned to him. "And that's not all, Collin. Our church would like to help you with your engine troubles, and even with some new tires . . ."

"Really?" He seemed a bit skeptical.

"Really," she said with a smile. "We had a special meeting last night. And everyone is behind this."

"Wow." He looked at Amy now. "I guess you were right after all."

"Right?" Edith wasn't sure what he meant.

"Oh, Amy kept telling me that you guys were good people. But after church last night, well, I just wasn't so sure."

Edith frowned slightly. "Well, some of our congregation can be a bit old-fashioned and hard to convince at times, but they basically have good hearts."

"That's just what I told Collin," said Amy. "I said we can't judge these people by appearances and that they probably thought we were pretty weird showing up in our bus like this—like from out of nowhere."

Edith smiled. "Yes, you've got that about right. In fact, I am curious as to where you came from and how you got this bus in the first place. It's not the sort of thing that one sees every day. At least not in Christmas Valley."

"The bus belonged to my dad," said Amy in a matter-of-fact tone. "But he didn't need it anymore. And we did." She held up her hand as if to say, "End of story."

"Oh." Edith looked around their cramped quarters again. "Well, come on in for breakfast whenever. You're welcome to use my laundry room if you'd like."

"That'd be great," said Amy. "I'm totally out of clean underwear." She laughed. "I'm actually wearing a pair of Collin's today. The funny thing is that they actually fit."

Edith wasn't quite sure how to respond to that, so she simply stood up and told them she had to get back before her cinnamon rolls burned.

10

At ten o'clock, after the last of the guests had finished breakfast, Edith called and informed Helen that the shower was a go.

"It sounds like they don't have much of anything," said Edith. "And living in the bus like that, without laundry facilities, well, I'm sure some extra clothes and blankets will come in handy."

"This is going to be fun," said Helen. "And I have all these decorations and plates and napkins and things that I'd wanted to use when Angie had her baby, and then her sister-in-law went and beat me to the punch."

"But that was more than twenty years ago, Helen."

"I know. But they were so cute that I hung on to them, and I plan to use them tomorrow."

"So you really think you can pull this off by tomorrow?"

"I don't see why not. People will come or they won't. But we *will* have a shower."

Not for the first time, Edith was reminded that Helen had once been a military nurse and that she was used to giving orders.

"Is ten o'clock all right with you?"

"It's fine."

"Great. I'll be there by 8:30 to set up."

"Be where?" Edith felt worried now.

"At the inn, of course. You didn't think I'd have it here, did you, Edith? Goodness knows, you've got far more room than I. And if you're not too busy, could you bake something yummy? You're such a good cook."

What could Edith say?

"And it might be easier if you made the punch too. Maybe something pink, since the decorations are blue and pink."

"Cake and punch," said Edith. "Anything else?"

"Well, do you happen to have mixed nuts and those little pastel mints on hand?"

"No, but I can get some."

"Oh, good. I think that should do it."

"How many people do you think we can count on, Helen?"

"Hmm . . ." Edith imagined her counting on her fingers. "I'd say at least twenty."

"Twenty?" Edith was surprised. "On such short notice? And just two days before Christmas?"

"Maybe even thirty."

Edith was not so sure. "Okay, well, I'll just make sure we have plenty, and if there are leftovers, I can use them during the holidays."

"Of course."

They said good-bye and hung up, and Edith just shook her head and sighed.

"What's wrong?" asked Charles as he came in to refill his coffee mug.

"Oh, nothing much. But it now looks as if I'm the one hosting the baby shower tomorrow."

"I thought Helen was taking care of everything."

"So did I. But it seems her way of taking care of it is to have it here."

He put a hand on her shoulder. "Poor Edith, you'll be ready for a vacation by New Year's."

She forced a smile. "Actually, I should be thankful. I'm very happy for Amy. And Helen has the hardest task anyway."

"What's that?"

She laughed. "Lining up guests who are willing to come to a shower for a girl they might not have met, who doesn't live here, and whose bright-colored bus is causing a bit of a fuss in town." Then she told him what the mayor had said.

"Don't worry about it, Edith. I'll talk to him. And I was just about to get Collin to come with me to get parts. We'll probably have to go out of town for them."

"Well, he's out shoveling snow," said Edith.

Charles smiled. "Good for him. Did you ask him, or did he just offer?"

"He just found the shovel and started doing it."

"And you think Amy will be okay here without him?" asked Charles with a slight frown. "I mean, if she should suddenly decide to go into labor and have her baby or need help or anything."

Edith laughed. "You sound just like an anxious father-to-be."

"Well, these kids seem a little helpless . . ."

"I know. And don't you worry. Amy's downstairs at the moment, doing several loads of
laundry. I'll be here. She should be just fine.
And if she should go into labor, there is always Helen."

He nodded. "Then I guess you're all in
good hands." He reached for his plaid wool
coat and went out the back door. Edith
watched him going out to speak to Collin,
who had nearly finished shoveling the sidewalk by now.

"Edith?" called a familiar voice. "Where
are you?"

"In the kitchen, Myrtle," Edith called back.

"Edith," said Myrtle as she came into the
kitchen, "you have a problem."

"And that would be?"

"There's a loose board on the stairs, and I
nearly fell and broke my neck just now."

Edith reached out and put a hand on Myrtle's fleshy forearm. "Are you okay?"

Myrtle, looking slightly indignant, pursed
her lips and said, "I think so. But it was quite
a scare."

"Oh, dear. I'm so sorry. Do you recall
which board it was?" Edith had come down
the stairs herself this morning but hadn't no-

ticed anything. Of course, Myrtle was quite a bit heavier, so it was possible that her weight had helped to loosen it.

"Second one from the top."

Edith looked out the window in time to see Charles and Collin driving away in the car. "Oh, dear," she said again. "I wonder if I could fix it myself."

Myrtle shook her head. "Not likely. You'll need to call in a handyman."

Edith considered this. Usually, she and Charles liked to do as much as possible for themselves, to spare their finances, but then again, if the board was really loose, she couldn't risk having a guest take a fall. "I'd better go look at it," she said suddenly. "And perhaps keep people off the stairs until it's fixed."

She saw Leslie and Megan just coming down the stairs now. "Did you notice a loose board up there?" she asked.

"As a matter of fact, I did," said Leslie. "It must've just happened, because I don't recall it wobbling like that before."

"Oh, dear. I better call a handyman right away." So Edith got on the phone and dialed Peter Simpson's number. Peter had occasionally helped them with bigger projects at the inn. As it turned out, Peter was not busy and promised to come right over. Edith hung up the phone and felt better.

"And what are you two doing today?" she asked Leslie and Megan. So far she'd been so busy with the other guests that she'd barely had a chance to talk to these two.

"I'm not sure," said Leslie, and Megan just shrugged. "We've already been to town to see Santa . . . and it's awfully cold out there today . . ."

"I have an idea," said Edith, leaning down to look into Megan's big blue eyes. "Do you like to decorate cookies?"

"With frosting and stuff?" Megan looked hopeful.

Edith nodded. "Yes, with frosting and stuff."

"Can I, Mommy?"

Leslie looked at Edith. "Are you sure? I mean, Megan hasn't had much experience with—"

"I'm sure by the time she finishes, Megan will be an expert. I have about eight dozen sugar cookies in the freezer, all ready to be decorated." Edith laughed. "Not that I expect Megan to do all of them."

Leslie smiled. "And if it's okay, maybe I could help her. I love doing creative things like that."

"Oh, it's better than okay. It would help me immensely. In fact, I was just about to invite you, as well as all the female guests at the inn, to come to a rather impromptu baby shower that I'm hosting tomorrow morning."

"A baby shower?" Megan clapped her hands and danced around. "I've always wanted to go to a baby shower. Can we, Mommy? Can we?"

Leslie just smiled. "I don't see why not." Then she looked at Edith. "But we'll have to get something for the baby. And I have no idea what to get. Is there a place in town with baby things?"

So Edith explained who the shower was for and that Rudolph's Five and Dime had a limited selection of baby things and Amy could probably use just about anything. "And can you come too, Myrtle?" she asked the older woman.

"I don't know . . . I still have a lot to do for the Christmas pageant. And besides," Myrtle frowned now, "I don't really like baby showers."

Megan looked at the old woman in disbelief. "You *don't* like baby showers? Why not?"

"Too many women in one room, and everyone yakking their heads off, all at once. Just gets on my nerves."

Edith tried not to look too relieved as she patted her on the shoulder. "Don't worry about it, Myrtle. I understand completely."

"I guess I could pick up something for the baby though." She grimly shook her head. "Poor child . . ."

"How about if Megan and I make a quick run to town now?" said Leslie with excitement in her voice. "We'll find something for the baby, then get back here to do cookies."

"Sounds like a great plan."

Edith posted a sign warning guests about the second stair tread and then went into the kitchen to get things ready for cookie decorating. She would cover the dining room table with waxed paper and just leave all the frostings and other tempting goodies out there in case any other guests wished to participate. It was the way she'd always done it with her own children, and usually, by the end of the day, the cookies were all decorated, although at final head count there were always quite a few missing in action.

After getting things ready for cookie decorating, Edith turned on her computer. She'd learned how to make cards at her last computer class, and so she found the right program, picked a baby graphic, and wrote out a very simple invitation that she neatly folded and addressed and slipped under the doors of all the women at the inn. Silly perhaps, since she'd already informed more than half of them. But it made the shower seem more special to go to this little bit of extra trouble. Amy emerged from the basement just as Edith was returning to the kitchen.

"Oh, do you need help?" offered Edith when she saw how off balance the very pregnant Amy looked while carrying a full basket of clean and folded clothes.

"I'm okay," said Amy. "But maybe you could get the door for me."

So Edith went ahead of Amy, opening and closing doors until they reached the bus, and this time it was not quite as laborious since Collin had made a clean path right up to the bus's door.

"Oh, yes," said Edith as she opened the door. "Charles and Collin went to get parts for the engine. I hope you don't mind."

"That's great." Amy smiled. "You guys are great. And I totally love your laundry room. You have so much counter space and stuff," she held the basket up proudly, "that I actually folded our clothes for a change. Collin will be surprised."

"That's nice."

"I still have one more load down there in the dryer, but my back was starting to ache so—"

"Don't worry about it. You go in there and have a little rest. We don't want you wearing yourself out, or going into labor, especially since your baby shower is scheduled for tomorrow morning."

Amy let out a happy squeal. "That is so totally cool!"

Edith nodded. "I'd better get back now." But as she walked back to the inn, heading for the front door to make sure that the steps had been properly de-iced, she couldn't help but agree with Amy. It was *so totally cool*!

Before Edith reached the front porch, she heard loud female voices arguing. They sounded as if they were coming from the direction of the church. She turned to see Myrtle and Olive, face-to-face, near the side door that led to the church kitchen, in what appeared to be some kind of standoff. She paused to watch them for a moment, and as the volume of their voices elevated, she grew seriously concerned that this argument might actually come to blows. She hurried across the street to see if she could help.

"You are not going to bring a bunch of stinking farm animals into this church!" shouted Olive. "I forbid it."

"Who died and made you God?" spat Myrtle.

"Edith!" exclaimed Olive when she saw her approaching. "Help me out with this lunatic."

"What's wrong?" asked Edith, fearing that she was already in over her head.

"This woman," said Olive dramatically, "wants to bring *live* animals into our church, the house of God—chickens and pigs and—"

"I *never* said pigs!" argued Myrtle. "I only thought it would make the pageant more interesting to have live animals, and I talked to a fellow on the phone this morning who said—"

"We are not going to have animals in church!" shouted Olive. "And the sooner you get that into your thick head, the better!"

"What makes you think that *you* get to make all the decisions?" demanded Myrtle with her feet spread apart and hands on hips.

"Because I'm the one in charge."

"Says who?"

Olive let out an exasperated groan and turned to Edith. "Please, Edith, do something! Or do I need to call Pastor Charles? This is really your fault, you know. Myrtle is your guest, and you've allowed her to help."

"So, she's been helping you?" asked Edith weakly.

"Helping me?" Olive practically shrieked. "With help like this, I might as well go out and hang myself."

"Oh, Olive . . ." Edith sighed. "There must be some way to resolve this."

"Yes!" said Olive. "And that's to tell her *no* farm animals." Then she turned and marched into the kitchen, slamming the door behind her.

"Are the children around?" asked Edith in a quiet voice.

"No," said Myrtle, still clearly unhappy. "They won't be here for another twenty minutes." Now she looked at Edith. "And how do you think the children would react to having live animals?" she asked. "Do you think they would enjoy feeling the nose of a fuzzy donkey or rubbing their hands through the thick curly wool of a sheep?"

Edith considered this. "Well, yes, I'd have to agree with you there, Myrtle. Kids love animals."

Myrtle smiled as if she had the upper hand now. "And if having animals around was good enough for the baby Jesus, I can't see how they could do much harm to a church, can you?"

"Well, no. Not actually . . . but then there's Olive . . . and she's dead set against it, Myrtle. And, really, she's the one who's supposed to be in charge. You're only supposed to be helping her." Edith was actually wringing her hands, something she hadn't done since childhood. "Please, Myrtle, can't you try to get along with her—for the sake of the children?"

Myrtle nodded. "This whole pageant is for the children, Edith. I won't do anything to ruin it for them."

"You won't?" Edith felt a smidgen of hope.

"Of course not. I want them to enjoy this time—and to remember it always."

"Oh, good." Edith glanced back to the inn just in time to see a small pickup parking in front. "I think my handyman is here now. I better go."

11

Within minutes, Peter had repaired the loose step and then headed off to the kitchen in search of Edith.

"All done," he announced.

Edith had just put in the last ingredients for tomorrow's shower cake. She'd decided to make it lemon with cream cheese frosting. And she would decorate it with pink and blue. Not terribly clever, but this was fairly last minute, and sometimes one just had to make do.

"Already?" she said as she turned on her big mixer and moved toward her little desk. "What do I owe you?"

Peter glanced around the kitchen, then grinned as his eyes spied something. "Are those cinnamon rolls?"

"Want one?" she offered.

"Got any coffee?"

"I do for you," she said. "Why don't you sit down and make yourself comfy."

"I can't believe that none of your kids came home for the holidays," said Peter. "If my parents' place was as great as this, I'd sure make the effort to go see them."

"How are your folks doing?" she asked as she set not one but two cinnamon rolls before him. "Do they like Arizona?"

"I guess. But I don't get it."

"Well, your mom said the winters here were getting to her. And then there was your dad's bypass surgery. You can't really blame them, Peter." She filled the coffeemaker with water.

"Maybe not. But when I get old, I don't plan on leaving. Christmas Valley is my home."

She smiled to herself as she imagined Peter old and gray but still tromping around town. "But you have to admit, it's not easy."

"Easy isn't always best," he said.

She turned on the coffeemaker and

turned off the mixer, glad to be rid of the extra noise. "Speaking of best, when are you going to start dating again, young man?"

He groaned. "You sound just like my mom."

"Well, it's a pitiful waste if you ask me, Peter. Just because your first wife didn't have the good sense to see that she got a great guy doesn't mean there's not someone else out there who would appreciate you."

"Not a whole lot of single women to pick from around here."

She considered this. At one time, she'd even tried to match Peter up with Krista, but that had turned into a disaster. "It was like going out with my own brother," Krista had told Edith afterward.

"Christmas Valley has its share of single women," she told Peter, trying to think of a single one that might appeal to him. "But perhaps none that are right for you."

"You got that right."

"How about some of those online matchmaking services? I get pop-ups and email ads from things like that all the time. Not that I need anything like that."

He laughed. "Somehow I just don't see myself as an online dating kind of guy."

She sneaked the still-brewing pot out and filled a mug, then set it down in front of him. "Well, maybe you should give it a try." She sat down across from him. "You're not getting any younger, you know, and it's awfully nice, as one gets older, to have someone beside you."

He nodded wistfully. "Can't disagree with you on that."

"Look, Mommy!" called a child's voice in the dining room. Edith was certain it was Megan. "Everything's all ready!"

"Let me put our stuff away first," called Leslie. "And you go wash your hands."

"Cookie day?" said Peter.

"Yes. Remember when you used to come over and help?"

"Those were good times."

"And sledding," she said with a sigh. "You kids had such fun at One Tree Hill."

"Yeah, and if your kids had had the good sense to come home, we'd be out there doing it again."

"Plenty of snow for it too." She stood up and went back to her desk now. "Seriously, Peter, what do I owe you for that stair?"

"You already paid me." He grinned at her. "And then some."

"Well, you take your time and finish up in here. I need to go out there and help them get all set. They're really doing me a big favor since I'm so busy just now. Those poor cookies probably never would've gotten decorated at all."

"And Christmas wouldn't be Christmas without Mrs. Ryan's famous Christmas cookies."

She laughed and went out to the dining room. Before long, she had Leslie and Megan all set, and it looked as if Leslie really knew what she was doing too. "I've got to go put a cake in the oven," she told them, "for the shower tomorrow." But before she could get back to the kitchen, she heard voices in the foyer, one that was definitely Myrtle's, and worried that Myrtle might be stirring up more trouble or getting into a flap with poor Mr. Benson, Edith decided to go see.

"Come on," Myrtle was saying, as it turned out, to Michael Thomas. "You won't be sorry."

"But I, uh . . ." Michael looked slightly helpless.

"Myrtle?" said Edith with a bit of a warning tone in her voice. "What are you doing?"

Myrtle turned around and gave Edith a sheepish expression. "Nothing . . ."

"Are you pestering Michael about—"

"She's fine," he said quickly, tossing Edith an assuring smile. "She's just trying to talk me into taking her somewhere in my car."

"Myrtle, please, don't be bothering the other guests."

"This is between me and Michael."

"I guess it couldn't hurt," he said now. "Lauren walked to town and won't be back for a while. I was just going to read and maybe catch a nap."

"You can nap anytime," said Myrtle.

Michael laughed. "I guess you're right."

Edith frowned. She didn't like the idea of Myrtle bullying the guests around. And she suspected that Myrtle had seen Michael's sporty little Porsche and just wanted to get him to take her for a joyride. Although how Myrtle was going to get her portly self in and out of that little car was a bit of a mystery.

"Have fun," said Edith, imagining Michael using a giant shoehorn to pry Myrtle from his car after they were done.

When Edith came back through the dining room, she was surprised to see that Peter had joined Leslie and Megan. He was bent over a toy soldier cookie and frosting him in what Edith could only imagine must be camouflage.

"Decided to help out?" she said.

"Do you mind?" he asked without looking up.

"Not at all. Did you introduce yourself to the ladies?"

He looked up now. "Of course. I told them that your kids and I used to do this every year, and Megan invited me to join them."

"And he's making G.I. Joe," said Megan, giggling.

"An untraditional Christmas cookie," he admitted, "but in honor of our armed forces."

"I think it's nice," said Leslie as she admired his work. "And it looks like real camouflage too."

"Peter is our local artist," Edith informed them.

"A real artist?" said Megan with big eyes.

"That's right," said Edith. "And he usually decorated the most interesting cookies too." Then she went into the kitchen to finish her cake making. Hopefully, the batter hadn't set too long. But it looked okay when she put the pans into the oven and even better when she took them out. Nice golden brown.

She set them on the counter to cool, then went upstairs to search for something. At least, she hoped she still had it. It was a baby quilt that she'd sewn for Tom and Alicia's last baby. Made from an adorable fabric that was covered with farm animals, the colors had been bright and bold. But then she'd heard that Alicia had chosen pastels for the nursery, and so Edith had put together a completely different quilt. She figured she'd have this one on hand for the next baby, and wasn't there always a next?

As far as she could remember, she hadn't given it away yet. After several minutes of intense hunting, she finally unearthed it in a plastic crate, along with a few other baby items. Things she'd probably gotten on sale for her own grandchildren, thinking that she would send them, or have them on hand when they came to visit her . . . and then, of course, she forgot all about them. Oh, well.

Since all seemed calm and quiet, for a refreshing change, Edith decided to take the time to wrap the baby gift, as well as to put up her feet. Already it seemed to have been a long day, or maybe the years were starting to catch up with her. Before she knew it, she had dozed off.

She awoke to what sounded like an urgent knocking on her door. "Edith?" called a female voice. "Are you in there?"

Thinking perhaps the inn was on fire, or worse, she stumbled to the door and opened it to see Lauren, Michael's wife, standing there. And she was clearly upset. "What's wrong?" asked Edith with a racing heart.

"It's Michael!" said Lauren breathlessly. "I went to town to get a gift for the baby shower, and he was going to have a nap while I was out, but now I get back and he's not in our room. And then I went downstairs and he's not down there, and his car's not here, and I'm just so—"

"It's okay," said Edith soothingly. "Michael simply took Myrtle for a little drive."

Lauren blinked. "A little drive?"

"That's right. Of course, it was all Myrtle's idea, but somehow she talked him into going. I'm sure she just wanted to have a ride in that pretty little car—"

Now Lauren burst into tears.

"It's okay," said Edith again. "Really, you don't need to be worried."

But Lauren just continued to sob, until Edith didn't know what to do, other than to guide her into the bedroom, something she had *never* done with a guest before. She sat Lauren down in the rocker, then sat herself down in Charles's recliner and waited for Lauren to recover. At first impression, Lauren had seemed a very together and controlled sort of person. A career woman, Edith had imagined, due to the classy business suit and leather briefcase. And certainly not the sort of woman who was given over to hysterics. Why should Lauren be so upset over Michael having gone somewhere with Myrtle—surely she couldn't be jealous of the heavyset woman who was old enough to be Lauren's grandmother? Finally, Lauren's sobs softened some, and Edith handed her a box of Kleenex.

"I'm so sorry," Lauren said as she blotted her face with a tissue. "I didn't mean to fall apart like that. It's just that I got so scared—it's like I knew that I'd lost him."

"You're a beautiful young woman," said Edith, still feeling confused. "I'm sure your husband would never leave you, and especially for someone, well, like Myrtle."

Lauren looked directly at Edith now, first with a shocked expression, but then she began to smile, and finally she actually laughed. Edith wondered what the joke was, but she didn't ask. She was just relieved to see Lauren happy.

"No, no . . ." said Lauren. "I didn't think that Michael had run off with—" she chuckled, "*Myrtle*, of all people. But, well, you see, the reason we came here for Christmas, rather than being with our families . . . oh, it's a long story."

"Well, you've aroused my curiosity," said Edith. "And I have time."

"And after all I've subjected you to, you probably deserve an explanation. Let me give you the short version. You see, Michael was diagnosed with and treated for cancer not long after we got married, about five years ago. And after all that time in remission and no symptoms, we believed that he was cancer free. We were even beginning to think about starting a family—" Her voice broke, and she looked down at her lap.

"But it came back?"

She nodded without speaking.

"And it's serious?"

She looked up. "Yes. They said there's no point in doing surgery and that they could try doing chemo, but it might just subject him to a lot of discomfort for no good reason. We just found this out a couple weeks ago, and we couldn't bear to be around family just yet. We didn't want to ruin everyone's Christmas, you know?"

"That was very selfless of you," said Edith. "But to be honest, if one of my children were sick, I would rather know."

"And we will tell them. We just wanted to wait until after Christmas. We also wanted to have this time together, just the two of us, to talk and think and sort it all out, you know?"

"And then Myrtle whisked your man away." Edith shook her head. "That woman!"

"Oh, it's okay. I mean, I know Michael wouldn't have gone with her if he didn't want to. Although why he would want to . . . well, I just can't imagine."

"I'm sure they'll be back soon."

"I'm sorry to burden you with this . . ."

"Please," said Edith, "don't be. You know, when we learned our kids weren't coming home, and when we decided to open the inn during Christmas, well, I just believed that the good Lord had a plan. And I'm sure you're part of that."

"Well, we really appreciate being here. And it's so great having a church so nearby. It's a real blessing." Lauren stood. "I'm going to go clean up my face before Michael gets back. Please, don't let him know that I fell apart on you."

"Of course not."

"Or that I told you about it."

"These lips are sealed."

"Thank you."

Of course, Edith felt like she could strangle Myrtle for enticing poor Michael to take her for a ride. And who knew when they'd be back. By now Myrtle could've convinced the poor man to take her, well, who knew where. And they were driving on snowy roads too. *Dear Lord, watch over them*, Edith prayed as she put on her shoes and went back downstairs.

At least Charles and Collin had gotten back. And, it appeared, with parts, since they were both outside, along with Peter now, looking into the engine of the bus.

"Peter knows how to fix cars," said Megan when she noticed Edith looking out the window.

"He sure does," said Edith. "He's good at fixing all kinds of things." She walked over to the table. "And how are our cookies coming?"

"Great," said Leslie, looking up from an angel-shaped cookie that she was transforming into something exquisitely celestial.

"Oh, my!" said Edith, examining the cookies that were already decorated. "I don't think we've ever had cookies this beautiful before. Are you an artist too?"

"Not exactly," Leslie admitted. "I mean, I like to dabble, but I'd never be able to support myself. But this," she held up the cookie, "is excellent therapy."

Edith smiled. "Well, I'm so glad you think so." Then she went in the kitchen to see if the cake layers had cooled yet.

"Hello there," called Charles as he came into the kitchen. "Sure smells good in here."

"Did you find everything you needed for the engine?" she asked as she mixed some frosting for the cake.

"For the engine. But we had to order the tires, and they won't be in until next week, after Christmas."

"Oh . . ."

"Now, don't worry, Edith. Hal Berry and I plan to do damage control in town this afternoon. We're going to talk to the mayor, during his Santa break, and try to make him understand that this is just a temporary problem. We'll also remind him that it wouldn't look good if the newspapers heard that we forced those poor kids to hit the road with bald tires on packed snow."

She smiled. "No, that wouldn't look good."

"And Hal has connections, you know." He winked at her. Hal's wife wrote the food column in their little weekly paper, and occasionally she sold a piece to one of the larger papers too.

"Sounds like you and Hal have it all taken care of."

"Peter offered to help Collin finish up out there." Charles was washing his hands in the sink now. "It gets a bit crowded with three heads under the hood. Besides, I was getting awfully cold. I think the temperature is dropping."

"Oh, I hope that Collin and Amy are warm enough in there."

"He said their noses get cold, but mostly they're fine."

"I'll take them out an extra comforter just in case."

"Yes, I figured you would, dear." He dried his hands. "I'm heading to town now. Anything you need?"

She gave him her short list of mints, nuts, and punch mix for the shower. Then, thinking twice, she took it back and wrote very specifically what kinds of mints, nuts, and punch mix.

"You know me well," he said as she handed it back.

That was true enough. Edith had learned from experience that if you simply wrote "mints," he might return with a small box of Junior Mints or mint-flavored gum. He was a smart man when it came to books and sermons, but he was at a complete loss in a grocery store.

It was getting dusky out when Collin and Peter came into the house by way of the kitchen, which was feeling more and more like Grand Central Station. Edith looked up from her task of trying to make the cake look like something fit for a baby shower.

"I think we got it," said Peter.

"Yeah," said Collin. "Peter's a genius."

Peter nodded. "Thank you, my man. It's nice that someone has finally noticed."

"Amy asked me to get a load of laundry for her," Collin said to Edith, and she directed him to the basement.

Now Peter seemed to be examining Edith's cake. "What is *that*?"

She frowned. "It was supposed to be a bassinet."

Peter laughed. "Looks more like a Volkswagen."

"Thanks a lot."

"You have any more of that pink and blue frosting?"

"Sure." She studied him. "You want to take a stab at it? I know you're more artistic than I am, but I don't want to see any soldiers in camouflage."

"I was thinking you should ask Leslie to help. She has a real knack."

Edith held her hands up. "Now, why on earth didn't I think of that? Go see if they're still out there. It's been so quiet, I think they might've finished."

Then Edith took her metal spatula and proceeded to scrape off the mess of blue and pink that she had created. Thank goodness she'd made plenty of frosting.

"I hear you need help?" said Leslie, standing in the doorway to the kitchen.

"That's right." Edith nodded toward the white-frosted cake.

But Leslie didn't make a move. Instead she pointed over her head. "The sign."

Edith laughed. "Goodness, I'd almost forgotten about that. Seems that no one's been paying attention to it lately anyway. Come on in."

Leslie came over and looked at the blank cake. "Peter's helping Megan to finish up the cookies. There's about a dozen left. So what did you have in mind for this?"

Edith shrugged. "Something babyish. I only mixed blue and pink frostings. I attempted a bassinet, but Peter said it looked like a Volkswagen. I think it looked more like a big blob. Anyway, I removed it. Do whatever you like with it. Judging by your cookie skills, I'm sure you'll have no problem."

12

"Seems quiet around here tonight," said Charles as he took a seat at the kitchen table.

"It's really settled down." Edith put the lid back on the boiling rice and turned the burner down to simmer. "It was getting pretty crazy earlier."

"I see only two places set," he observed. "Where's our friend Myrtle tonight?"

Edith just shook her head. "You're not going to believe it."

"Try me."

"Well, Leslie and little Megan had been helping me to decorate cookies, and then

Leslie even did the decoration on the cake for the shower tomorrow—and what a beautiful job she did! But anyway, we were just finishing things up, and Myrtle walked in and asked Leslie and Megan what they were doing for dinner. At first I thought maybe she was going to invite them to join us, which would've been okay, actually, they'd been so helpful and all."

"So Myrtle went to dinner with Leslie and Megan?"

"Yes, she pretty much invited herself, and then she even invited Peter."

"Peter?" Charles looked confused.

"Peter had been helping with the cookies too, and he was still here. So the four of them went to dinner together."

"Interesting . . ." Charles smiled.

"Oh, yes, and Peter told me to tell you that the engine is running just fine now. Collin called him a genius."

"And how is our little mother-to-be?"

"I think she wore herself out doing laundry today. Her back's been hurting, and she's been resting. I took them out a comforter and some dinner. And they were very sweet and grateful." She sadly shook her head.

"But that bus! Oh, it may look bright and cheery on the outside—in fact, I've started calling it the Christmas bus—but on the inside it's downright depressing. And not very warm either, especially with the temperature dropping. They have this little heater that they run off a battery, but it can only be on for short periods of time."

"I wonder if we could run an extension cord out there," mused Charles. "Plug it in the outlet on the front porch."

"That might work, well, as long as no one tripped over it. That Myrtle gave me a good scare today when she said she tripped on the loose step. I thought this could turn into a lawsuit for sure. And wouldn't Myrtle be the one to do it?"

"Oh, I don't know . . ."

Edith knew this was his gentle way of defending Myrtle. But that's just how he was. Charles never liked to say a bad word about anyone. And normally, she didn't either. She checked on the poached fish and decided it was done.

Then she decided to tell him about Lauren's emotional breakdown and confession after Myrtle hijacked Michael earlier that day, not so much to shine a negative light on Myrtle as to bring Michael's illness to Charles's attention.

"That's too bad."

"I have absolutely no idea what Myrtle was up to, but it really upset poor Lauren."

"But he made it back okay?"

"Yes, he actually seemed in really good spirits, and he and Lauren went off to dinner and the Christmas play tonight. They were having a double date with the Fieldses, if you can imagine. Unfortunately, the Fieldses got into another argument just as they were leaving. Hopefully, they'll settle down."

"Might help Lauren and Michael to be thankful for what they have . . ." Charles said, "even if it is going to be cut short."

She smiled at him as she set the rice on the table. "You know, I'd rather have a few wonderful years with love than a long life with animosity."

"Well said, my dear."

She put the rest of the food on the table and removed her apron.

"And how about Mr. Benson?"

"He told me that he'd had an early dinner in town and wanted to just stay in and read."

"Poor old guy. This is his first year without his wife, and he's feeling very lost."

"So that's why he's so sad," she said as she sat down. "And then he's got Myrtle pestering him almost nonstop. I just don't understand that woman. It's as if she cannot keep her nose out of everyone's business."

"Takes all kinds, my dear."

"I just hope she doesn't spoil dinner for those kids tonight."

Then Charles bowed his head and asked a blessing. He also took a few moments to pray that their guests might have a good evening. Despite her concerns for the young people subjected to Myrtle's unpredictable prattle, Edith couldn't help but relish this quiet dinner with just Charles and her. And as they ate, he filled her in on the details in town today. It seemed that he and Hal had made some headway.

"I think Mayor Drummel is softening up about the bus," he finally said. "In the spirit of Christmas."

"Oh, and I almost forgot to tell you. The strangest thing . . . people have been stopping by to look at the bus. Can you imagine it? As if it's some kind of sideshow attraction.

Peter said that at one point there were at least half a dozen out there just looking at it."

Charles laughed. "This is a small town, Edith. Word gets around."

"You'd think people would have more to do, just three days before Christmas, than to stand around gaping at an old bus."

After cleaning up the dinner things, Charles went off to his study, and Edith went down to put a load of linens into the washing machine. She normally did this in the morning, but what with the baby shower and all, she figured she might as well get ahead of the game. She was pleased to see that her laundry room was in good shape. Amy had even cleaned the lint out of the lint trap, something her own children usually forgot to do. Edith didn't like to admit it, but she was meticulous about laundry and her laundry room. Normally, like her kitchen, it was off-limits to guests. But then rules were made to be broken. And perhaps it was good for Edith to bend a bit.

When Edith came up from the basement, she heard voices in the dining room. As usual, she had put out refreshments for guests to help themselves to—well, even more so since it was the holidays. And she wasn't surprised that people were out there, but she was surprised that it sounded like Myrtle.

"Don't you know that'll send your cholesterol sky-high?" she was saying in that know-it-all tone she so often used.

Edith paused on the other side of the door, not exactly eavesdropping since this was her own home, after all, but she was curious as to who Myrtle was talking to.

"My cholesterol is *my* business," said a voice that sounded like Mr. Benson's.

"And coffee before bed?" she said. "Do you know what caffeine can do to your blood pressure?"

"It's *my* blood pressure."

"It won't be for long if that's the best you can take care of yourself."

Edith was just about to break it up, but his next sentence stopped her.

"Look, woman." His voice grew louder. "Maybe I don't care about *that*. Maybe I don't *want* to be here for long."

"Tsk, tsk. That's no way to talk, Mr. Benson. It was the good Lord who put you on this planet, and it's up to the good Lord to decide when it's time for you to go. Don't you know that much by now?"

"All I know is that you're the most exasperating human being I've ever run across, and I wish you'd mind your own business!"

"How do you know that it isn't my business? People are supposed to help people. What kind of a world would it be if everyone just turned their backs and walked away?"

"It would be a much happier world for me!"

Edith couldn't take any more. She pushed open the door and walked out, pretending that she'd heard nothing. With a forced smile, she turned her attention to Myrtle, asking how dinner with the young people had gone.

"It was fine," she answered quickly, still appearing to have her sights set on poor Mr. Benson. Edith was surprised that he was even still here, but he was standing by the table, his face flushed and brows drawn tightly together. He had a plate with a large slice of pumpkin pie and whipped cream in one hand and a cup of coffee in the other. He reminded Edith of a trapped animal.

"Would you like to sit down?" offered Edith.

"Thank you." He seemed relieved to have someone else in the room.

"Where are Leslie and Megan?" Edith

asked Myrtle, hoping she might distract her from this relentless attack on Mr. Benson.

"They decided to go see the play."

"Good for them." Edith cut herself a thin slice of pumpkin pie and topped it with a dollop of whipped cream. She wasn't all that fond of pumpkin pie, but after Myrtle's comments about cholesterol, she wanted to do this as an alliance with Mr. Benson. Then she poured a cup of tea and went over to sit across from him, keeping an eye on Myrtle as she did.

"Aren't you having anything, Myrtle?" she asked.

"I can't decide."

Edith made light conversation with Mr. Benson as she watched Myrtle standing by the dessert table. She spoke of the weather, town happenings, and the Christmas pageant that would take place the next night, and after a bit she sensed the old man was beginning to relax.

"I haven't seen a Christmas pageant in years," he said wistfully. "I remember when I was a boy and I got to play the shepherd once."

"Myrtle is helping with the pageant," Edith told him, feeling a bit guilty, not to mention inhospitable, for not including her in the conversation as well.

"That's right," said Myrtle as she finally poured herself a cup of herbal tea and placed two small pieces of divinity on a plate. Edith had to smile to herself at this healthy choice, since she already knew that Myrtle ate things loaded with fats and sugar.

Myrtle sat down at the end of the table. "And tomorrow will be a very busy day. I wish I could talk someone into driving me to town. There are a few props that I still need to pick up at the hardware store."

"I'm pretty busy with the baby shower," Edith said.

Now Myrtle looked hopefully at Mr. Benson. "I don't suppose you'd want to help out . . . especially after I gave you such a bad time about taking care of yourself." She looked down at her plate now. "I'm sorry."

Edith blinked in surprise. This was the first apology she'd heard from Myrtle.

Mr. Benson cleared his throat. "I guess I shouldn't be so touchy."

"And I shouldn't be so bossy. People tell me that all the time. But it's just my nature."

"The truth is, you're right about the cholesterol and the high blood pressure."

Myrtle gave a little victory nod that made her double chins wobble.

"My wife always tried to get me to watch what I ate. And I did just fine while she was around. But after she died last year . . . well, it's just not easy."

"And how do you think your wife would feel to know that you've thrown your diet to the wind?"

He sighed.

"So how about giving me a ride to town tomorrow?" she said. "It can be your contribution to the Christmas pageant."

And to Edith's flabbergasted surprise, Mr. Benson actually agreed. Whether this was a calculated and well-executed plan in Myrtle's strange mind or just a crazy fluke, Edith wasn't sure. But she couldn't help but think that Myrtle was a bit of a manipulator.

"If you'll excuse me, I need to go put some things in the dryer," Edith said, standing. She figured her job as referee was over. Surely these two wouldn't kill each other now.

"That's some good pie," said Mr. Benson as he set his fork on his now-empty plate. "But if you'll excuse me," he nodded to both of them, "I'd like to say good night."

"Thank you and good night." Edith was

gathering a few empty dishes from the table to take with her to the kitchen.

But Mr. Benson was barely out of sight before Myrtle got up and helped herself to a generous piece of pumpkin pie and whipped cream. When she saw Edith watching, she just smiled sheepishly. "Just trying to set a good example for the old guy," she said as she sat down and began to eat.

Edith chuckled as she went into the kitchen and set the small stack of dessert plates in the sink. Of course, she had to wonder about Myrtle's cholesterol levels and blood pressure. Not that she would dare mention it!

By the time Edith finished with the laundry, the house was quiet. She put the perishable foods into the refrigerator but left a nice selection of cookies and treats on the table, in case any guests were in need of a midnight snack. Then she unplugged the Christmas tree lights and blew out the candles that she had lit earlier in the evening. But as she bent over to blow out the large white pillar candle in the foyer, something gave her pause. Something wasn't right.

She studied the shiny holly with its red berries that gracefully wreathed around the candle, reflected in the glossy finish of the smooth mahogany tabletop, and finally she knew what was wrong—her porcelain angel was gone. She searched around the foyer, by the registration area, then in the living room, and finally she stopped at Charles's study. The light was showing beneath the door, so she suspected he was in there.

"Hello?" she said quietly as she opened the door.

He looked up and sort of blinked, almost as if he'd been asleep, but she suspected he'd simply been immersed in his book. Charles loved reading old-fashioned western novels. Of course, he'd read every one he could get his hands on over the years, but claiming his memory was fading with age, he had started reading them all over again. If he ever got Alzheimer's, God forbid, he would probably be happy just reading the same one over and over again.

"Sorry to bother you."

He smiled and closed the paperback. "You know that's never the case."

"Have you seen my angel?"

He looked puzzled.

She smiled. "The porcelain angel that I keep in the foyer. It seems to be missing."

He scratched his head. "I do remember that angel. Very pretty. But I have no idea where she may have flown off to."

Edith frowned. "Do you think someone might've accidentally bumped into it and broken it?" She remembered how taken Megan had been with the pretty sculpture, how she had almost touched it until her mother stopped her.

"Without mentioning it?"

"That does seem unlikely." She thought about it for a moment. "You don't think anyone took it, do you?"

"I can't imagine why."

"Well, it actually is a fairly valuable piece."

"Really?"

She kind of shrugged now, sorry that she'd even said that. "Not that anyone would be aware of its value . . . besides me."

He leaned forward with interest now. "I suppose I've never asked you—it just seems it's always been around—but where did the angel come from, Edith?"

She sat down in a chair across from him. "My grandmother."

"Oh . . ."

Now, Charles knew as well as anyone that Edith still had some regrets about her grandparents. But he never pried. "She gave it to me for my sixteenth birthday," Edith told him. "Of course, she also informed me that it was an expensive piece that would get more valuable with time. And she told me not to break it." Edith made a meek smile. "I was rather clumsy as a kid."

"Because you were tall for your age."

"Yes."

"So where do you think your angel is, Edith?"

She shook her head. "I have no idea. This has been such a busy day with people coming and going. But I think if someone had accidentally broken it, I would've heard something, don't you think?"

He nodded.

"Do you think someone has taken it?" She hoped this was not the case.

"I sure wouldn't like to think that."

"No, no . . ." she said quickly. "Neither would I."

"Maybe it will turn up."

"Yes. I'm sure it will."

Just the same, Edith felt a gnawing concern growing inside of her. Could it be that someone had actually stolen her angel? And, if so, who? A lot of people had been in and out of the inn today. Of course, she knew that most people would point their fingers at someone like Collin or Amy—they were virtual strangers and obviously in financial need. But Edith couldn't believe that they would do that, not after all the kindness Edith and Charles had shown them. She refused to believe it.

13

Edith rose early on Friday morning. There was so much to be done that she needed a head start. She'd already started composing a detailed list in her head, and hopefully, she could get it all down onto paper before she forgot anything. But as she walked through the foyer, she paused by the mahogany table. Last night, while in bed, she had wondered if perhaps she had imagined the whole thing, if she would get up in the morning and the angel would be in its proper place. But it was not there. She even took a moment to look closely at the wooden floor, actually running her fingers over the surface just in case there was a fragment of broken porcelain. But other than a day's worth of dust, the floor was clean.

She tried not to let it get to her as she went into the kitchen, sat down at her desk, and made out her list of tasks. And she tried not to think about it while she sat and read her daily devotional. But as she went around doing her regular morning chores, she thought not only about the missing angel, but also about her grandmother. She wasn't having the usual memories about her grandmother, the negative ones. Instead she was remembering some of the good things. It was her grandmother who had first taught her to rise early. And to make lists. And even as Edith measured the ingredients for Belgian waffles, she remembered that it was her grandmother who had taught her to cook and sew and keep house. Although her grandparents had been wealthy enough to pay someone else to do those things, her grandmother had always been very thrifty and frugal and insisted on doing them for herself. "It's from my childhood," she had told Edith once. "My mother was from the old country, and she taught us to make do."

And as Edith went about her daily tasks, she realized more and more how much her grandmother had influenced her—and she realized how much of it was good.

For the first time that she could remember, Edith realized that she really did love and appreciate her grandmother. And her soft-spoken grandfather too. And she truly was thankful that they had taken her in after her parents were killed in a car wreck when Edith was just a toddler. Certainly they were old-fashioned and a bit set in their ways, but then they were old, probably too old to have been raising a child. But, she now knew, they had always had her best interests at heart. Why hadn't she seen that sooner?

Goodness, she hoped no tears had fallen into the batter while she stirred. She set the big bowl aside and went to wipe her wet face on a dish towel. Even as she did this, she knew that these were not bitter tears. They were simply tears of release. Letting go. Accepting things for what they were and finding something to be thankful for in the process.

By the time she had breakfast ready to serve, she felt as if the tears had cleansed something in her. And even if she never saw that porcelain angel again, she knew that it had done its work.

"Need any help?" asked Charles as he came in from his walk and hung up his coat and scarf.

She was already pouring him a cup of coffee. "No, I think it's all under control." She wanted to tell him about her little epiphany in regard to her grandmother but figured that could come later. When life wasn't so busy. For now she just needed to stay on track, get breakfast served and cleaned up, and then help Helen set up things for the shower.

Edith had suspected that Mr. Benson would have second thoughts about playing chauffeur to Myrtle today. After all, she'd sort of bullied him into it last night. Edith wasn't surprised to hear them talking about it as she set a platter of fruit on the table.

"I'm sorry, but I don't think it's a good idea," he was telling Myrtle.

"You're not backing out on me, are you?" Her bulldog face was set.

"I just think—"

"I would've taken you as a man of your word," she said.

"Oh, well, fine," he huffed. "I'll drive you, then."

Edith tried not to laugh as she went back to the kitchen for more waffles. Poor Mr. Benson. He didn't have a chance against the likes of Myrtle Pinkerton.

Edith tried not to act as if she was hurrying her guests, but to her great relief the last of them departed the dining room before nine o'clock, giving her just enough time to whisk the breakfast things off into the kitchen. She'd already sent Helen to the living room, where they would have the shower, to decorate or rearrange chairs or whatever it was she felt needed to be done.

The inn's male guests, probably sensing that they were not particularly welcome at a baby shower, made themselves scarce. And the female guests actually offered to help. Little Megan was literally dancing with joy as she watched streamers of blue and pink crepe paper being hung in the doorway.

By ten o'clock the shower guests began to arrive. Mostly ladies from church, but also a few from Helen's bridge group, and even the mayor's wife made a showing. Along with the guests from the inn (excluding Myrtle, who was noticeably absent—at least to Edith, who had simply breathed a sigh of relief), there was a grand total of twenty-three women present! Not bad, thought Edith as she placed another gift on the impressive pile, especially considering how Amy was a complete stranger to most of them and it was only two days until Christmas. Of course, Edith suspected that some of these women had come out of plain old curiosity. They'd probably heard talk in town and wanted to see what kind of people inhabit a wild-looking bus like the one parked in front of the inn. And others, possibly pressured by Helen, one of the town's leading socialites, had probably been afraid to say no.

Helen, limping around with her cane in hand, played the gracious hostess by greeting everyone, introducing them to Amy, and finally coaching the women through some familiar shower games, complete with prizes. The napkins and plates and things, older than Amy, were old-fashioned but sweet. And everyone thought the cake decorating was outstanding—a frilly pink and blue bassinet that looked nothing like a Volkswagen. Edith told them it was Leslie's doing.

"You should stick around," said Betty Gordon, owner of the Candy Cane Shoppe. "I could use someone like you in my business." Leslie laughed and said she couldn't imagine living anywhere as charming as Christmas Valley. Of course, this pleased the ladies, especially the mayor's wife, who took any compliment to their town as personal praise.

Amy, Edith felt certain, was overwhelmed when it was time to open the gifts. But she kept a sunny smile on her face and said thank you about a hundred times. She did get some nice and much-needed baby things, especially considering the short notice. But it wasn't long, barely an hour, before women began to excuse themselves, saying, "I still have gifts to wrap . . ." or "I'm not done baking . . ." Edith began to think that having a baby shower just days before Christmas was actually rather brilliant as she handed women their coats and thanked them for coming.

Olive was standing next to her, reminding everyone about the Christmas pageant as they went out the door. "The children have been working so hard," she said. "You all be sure to come."

Edith felt bad for Olive. Local interest in the Christmas pageant had been in a steady decline for the past several years, and that was when Judy had been managing it. She just hoped Olive wouldn't be too disappointed if the church was only half full tonight.

Finally the last of them left, including Helen, still leaning on her cane as she carefully made her way down the porch steps, with Edith steadying her from the other side. The last thing Edith wanted was for Helen to take another spill on the slippery path.

"Thanks for doing this for Amy," Edith said as they walked. "It was really wonderful."

Helen smiled. "It was, wasn't it?"

"And now Amy is all ready to have her baby."

"Well, let's just hope she's not too ready. But if anything happens, you make sure you call me."

"Do you really mean that, Helen? I mean, you've got your bad knees and all. Not that I think Amy is going to go into labor. Hopefully, the baby will wait until they get to California."

They were at Helen's car now, and Helen turned to look at her. "I do mean it, Edith. You know that Dr. Martin is out of town, and I've delivered babies before. Although why Amy wants to do a home birth, or should I say *bus birth*, is beyond me."

"They don't have insurance," Edith reminded her. "Plus they're nearly broke."

"I know that. But everyone knows how lots of uninsured people take advantage of hospitals without the wherewithal to pay for it. Not that I approve of that, mind you."

"Maybe Collin and Amy have more scruples than that."

Helen laughed. "You wouldn't know that to look at them, now would you?"

"Do you think that's what folks might've said about Mary and Joseph when they came to town, road weary and dusty, looking for a place to stay?"

"I don't know about that, but you can tell our little Amy to get plenty of rest. I think the festivities might've worn her out. And knowing she hasn't had proper prenatal care is a big concern to me. Insurance or no insurance, that young woman should see an obstetrician before the baby comes."

"I don't know what we can do about that. But I'll encourage her to rest and take it easy."

But Edith didn't need to tell Amy to rest. Collin had already come in to collect Amy along with all the baby things, and they were heading out to the bus as Edith came in.

"That was fun," Amy told Edith. "But my back's killing me. I'm going to go lie down for a while."

"Good for you."

"Thanks again for everything," Amy called as she and Collin slowly made their way out the back door.

Edith was surprised that Collin didn't say anything to her. Not even a thank-you for the baby things, which were for his child. And suddenly thoughts of the missing angel flashed through her mind again, but as quickly as they came she dismissed them. It would do no good to dwell on it or to wrongly blame someone like Collin. Like Charles had said, the missing angel would probably show up in time.

By midafternoon, Edith realized that she was actually ahead of herself today. Things from the shower were all cleaned up, daily chores at the inn were complete, and she even had a roast in the Crock-Pot. So she decided to take this time to write her kids a short note on email. She usually did this every other day or so, but due to the busy-ness at the inn, she was a few days behind. To her delight, she had correspondence from each of them—including Krista, in Maui. All of them expressed sadness about not being home for Christmas. But they had all received their packages, except Krista since she'd already left the mainland, al-though, Edith suspected by Krista's ebullient email, being in Maui probably made up for it.

She took her time reading each letter and even printed out the pictures that some of them had sent to show to Charles. Edith still marveled at this new age of technology. But she was thankful to have photos of nine-year-old Jessica's Christmas recital; Jame-son dressed up like Santa, with a lopsided beard, for his kindergarten Christmas pro-gram; and baby Allison in her red velvet dress. And, of course, there was Krista standing by a palm tree, looking cute as a button in her bright-colored sundress. Edith hoped she remembered to use sunblock. Krista always burned so easily.

Edith heard voices in the inn as she hit the send button on a rather long letter that she'd written to all four of her kids, telling of the comings and goings at the inn, promising to write more later, and ending the letter with, "It's not exactly like having my own dear children home with me at Christmas, but it has been interesting. Love always, Mom." Then she turned off the computer and went out to see who was here.

"Oh, there you are," said Myrtle. "Didn't you hear me calling you?" She was setting two large bags from the hardware store on the dining room table.

Mr. Benson put two more beside them. He glanced at Edith and made a slight eye-rolling gesture, as if he'd had it with Myrtle. "Now, if you ladies will excuse me," he said in a tightly controlled voice, "I'd like to go have a rest in my room."

"Of course," said Edith, feeling sorry for the beleaguered man.

Myrtle just shook her head. "Good grief, I didn't force him to go."

Edith decided not to tackle that one. "What are these?" She nodded to the bags cluttering her pretty dining room table.

"For the pageant," Myrtle said as if that explained everything.

"Why don't you leave them at the church?"

"Olive might not like it."

Now Edith was curious. "Mind if I take a look?"

"No. It's only to make it more realistic. You know they didn't have electricity two thousand years ago."

Edith peeked in a bag to see that it contained some kerosene lanterns and a bottle of kerosene. She frowned as she imagined young children burning their fingers, or the church possibly going up in flames. "Don't you think this might be a little dangerous in the church?"

"They're not for in the church. It's for later."

"Later?"

"Yes, *later.*"

"Meaning you're not going to let the children use these in the church during the Christmas pageant tonight?" Edith wanted to be perfectly clear.

"Right."

"So, why did you get them?"

Myrtle just waved her hand. "Oh, you'll see. Look, I've still got lots to do before the day is over, and my feet are killing me. I need to go put them up for a while." And she walked away, leaving the four hardware store bags on the table.

Edith just shook her head, then stowed

the bags in a small storage closet beneath the stairs. Perhaps Myrtle would forget about the lanterns, since it didn't seem that she had much use for them, and something that hazardous certainly wasn't going to be allowed in the church. What was that woman thinking anyway?

14

"Edith?" His voice had a sound of urgency in it.

"In here, Charles," she called from the kitchen, where she was packaging up some cookies for the pageant.

"Have you seen *this*?" he said as he came through the door.

"What?" She turned to see what he was talking about, and it seemed he had some sort of flyer in his hand.

"This!" He thrust the flyer at her, then ran his hands through his hair, a gesture he reserved for only the most frustrating of times. Usually it had to do with their children getting into mischief or something that had gone seriously wrong at church. It'd been a while since she'd seen him do it.

She studied the pale green paper with handwritten letters. Not very professional looking, almost as if a child had done it. It seemed to be an announcement in regard to the pageant tonight. But it also said that live animals would be involved and that they were having a live nativity afterward and everyone was invited. At the bottom of the flyer was a rough-looking sketch of what appeared to be a manger scene, although the donkey looked more like a miniature elephant. Or maybe it was supposed to be an ox.

"A live nativity?" he said. "Live animals? No one told me."

"Well, Olive and Myrtle had been arguing about some such thing, but I'm fairly certain that Olive has this under control."

"Then where did these come from?"

"I don't know." Of course, she had a pretty good idea. "It looks as if a child may have done it . . . or perhaps Myrtle."

"Where is that woman?"

Unused to him using that tone, she felt slightly alarmed. "Now, Charles, we can't go blaming her if we don't even know that she's responsible."

He sank down into a kitchen chair. "I know, dear. You're right. It's just that everyone in town is talking about this and the bus, and then, of course, there's Myrtle. I'm sure they think we're all crazy. What am I going to do?"

She put her hand on his shoulder. "I'm sure you'll think of something."

"You know Olive has been hinting that I'm getting too old to pastor a church," he said in dismay. "She's insinuating that I'm losing it, out of touch . . . and now this. I'm afraid she may be right."

"No, dear, she's not right. It's just that, well, things have been a little odd lately." She kind of laughed. "And it all seemed to shift right after you did your wonderful sermon about showing hospitality."

He nodded. "Well, maybe the good Lord has a hand in this. But, seriously, what do you think I should do?"

She considered this. "Well, if you ask Olive about it, she might just get upset. I think Myrtle's up in her room. Maybe we should start there." So they went upstairs and knocked on Myrtle's door, but no one answered. Edith looked at her watch. It was nearly four. "Well, Myrtle did tell me she had a lot to do today. I'm not sure what that means, but—"

"Anything wrong?" asked Michael as he and Lauren came up the stairs.

"No," said Edith. "We're just looking for Myrtle."

Michael nodded and smiled as if perhaps he knew something, but he didn't say anything.

"Do you know where she is?" asked Charles.

Michael kind of grimaced now. "Well, I do . . . but I'm not supposed to tell."

"Michael?" said Lauren. "What are you talking about?"

"It has to do with that little car trip we took yesterday."

"Yeah?" Lauren continued the questioning.

"Well, she made me promise not to tell."

Charles held up the green flyer. "Does it have anything to do with this?"

Michael made a funny little smile that seemed to confirm this. "But don't worry, she's got everything all worked out. We actually had a lot of fun setting things up and, well, I really can't say anything more, but it should be a great evening—if all goes well."

"If all goes well?" repeated Charles in a weak voice. "Meaning that it might not?"

"Really, Pastor Charles," Michael assured him. "It's like you said in church Wednesday night. It's all just a matter of trust."

Charles nodded. "Yes, I suppose you're right."

But Edith wasn't so sure. Oh, it wasn't that she didn't trust God. She did. It was just Myrtle who worried her. She considered telling Charles about the lanterns but thought better of it. Poor man had enough on his mind already.

As they went downstairs, he just shook his head. "Well, maybe I need to just take my hands off this," he said. "It's not as though I'm the one responsible for the pageant. That's why I delegate things . . . but sometimes . . ." He turned and looked at Edith. "And as soon as I call Hal Berry and ask him to go remove all these flyers from town, I think I will remain in my study to pray about this matter."

She smiled. "That sounds like a wise plan. Dinner will be ready around five so that we'll have plenty of time to, uh, help with the pageant—just in case it's needed." Edith hadn't "helped" with the pageant in years. It had been such a relief when her children were too old for it and she was able to pass the responsibility to another. Then Judy got involved, and Edith had never really given it a second thought, until this year.

Thinking of Judy gave Edith an idea. Surely Judy and her family would be in Christmas Valley by now. Hadn't Olive said they were coming in time to see the pageant? Perhaps she could give Judy a call and give her a little heads-up about what might or might not happen tonight. She dialed Olive's number, and to her relief, Judy answered. After dispensing with cordialities, Edith got right to the point. "Judy, I wanted to let you know that there could be a slight problem at the pageant tonight."

"Does this have to do with the animals?"

"How did you know?"

"Mother and I were in town, and she saw a flyer and went ballistic. She's on her way to the church now. I'm sure you'll see her in a few minutes. She's looking for some crazy lady named Myrtle. But, honestly, it sounded so weird that I thought maybe she was making it up or getting senile. Who is this Myrtle person?"

Edith tried to explain but saw the futility. "The main reason I called, Judy, was to ask for your help tonight, I mean if things should get a little, well, you know . . ."

"Crazy?"

"Yes. I spoke to another guest, and he seems to have some inside information that it is entirely possible that Myrtle has arranged for real animals to be involved tonight. How she managed this, God only knows. But I hate the idea of seeing your mother being, well, stressed out—and then there are the children, and well . . ."

"I understand, Edith. And I do plan to be on hand. And if you want to know the truth, I think the idea of having live animals is rather charming. I even considered it myself one year, but it was so overwhelming that I finally gave up. If your Myrtle can pull this off, I'm happy to do what I can to keep things running smoothly."

"You're a saint!"

Judy laughed. "I'm glad you think so. My mother may have a fit if she finds out I'm in support of this."

"Well, it's more about being in support of

the children, don't you think? This is their night, really. I just don't want it spoiled for them."

"I understand."

Edith felt much better after she hung up. She would reassure Charles whenever he emerged from his study. No sense in interrupting his prayer, since she was certain they'd all need it before this night was over.

"Edith?"

She knew it was Olive. Taking a deep breath, she went out to meet her.

Olive had a flyer in her hand and a look of rage on her face. And before Edith could get out a word, Olive began. "What is going on? Is this Myrtle's doing? Where is that woman?"

"Olive," Edith said in her best calming voice. "Come into the kitchen and sit down. I just made a pot of peppermint tea, and I think you could use a cup." She reached for her coat. "Let me take that for you."

"Edith!" Olive exclaimed as Edith wrestled her for her coat. "This is serious."

"Come sit down." They were in the kitchen now, and while Olive continued to rant about what a total catastrophe this evening would be, Edith busied herself with tea and a plate of goodies.

"I swear, unless someone arrests Mad Myrtle and puts her safely in jail, we are all doomed tonight."

"Oh, Olive." Edith set the cookie plate and tea in front of her. "I think you're overreacting."

"Overreacting?"

"Look, if it makes you feel any better, Charles and I both plan to be on hand to help out, to keep things under control. And I've even lined up some other helpers." Edith didn't want to mention the phone call to Judy. It might make Olive feel badly, as if she were unable to keep this thing under control herself. "And I'm sure it's going to be just fine."

"But what about this flyer?" Olive said, waving the paper in the air like a surrender flag. "What about everyone in town who's seen these?"

"First of all, Hal Berry is probably down there right now, taking them all down. But second of all, you know how much attention people pay to flyers, especially this time of year. And these don't even look like anything official. I doubt that anyone even took them seriously."

"You really think so?" Olive looked slightly hopeful as she picked up her teacup.

"Yes, I do. Furthermore, Charles is in his study right now praying for this whole evening to go well."

"Hmm." Olive didn't seem particularly moved by this. "Might do more good if he came out and put Mad Myrtle in her place."

Edith wanted to ask Olive to refrain from calling their guest Mad Myrtle, but sometimes one had to choose one's battles. "Myrtle isn't here."

"Oh?"

"I don't know where she is."

"Well, she wasn't at church. I checked there first. Do you think she's left? Perhaps gotten scared that she stepped over the line and just taken off with her tail between her legs?"

Edith shrugged. "I have no idea."

They finished their tea, and Olive, somewhat subdued, said she had things to get ready at the church.

"I'm bringing cookies over," said Edith. "Do you want me to stay and help?"

Olive waved her hand. "No, barring any visits from Mad Myrtle, I should be just fine. But if you hear screaming from across the street . . ."

"Olive!" Edith gave her a warning look.

"Kidding."

Charles and Edith had just finished dinner when Edith noticed a large truck parked across the street. Other than Collin and Amy's bus, which was strange enough, or the occasional moving van, she was unaccustomed to seeing large trucks in this neighborhood. Edith went into the living room to look out the big picture window.

"It could be a farm truck," she told Charles, seeing that he was coming too.

"Can you see anything else?" he asked as he joined her.

"Not really. The truck is pretty much blocking everything."

"I'm going over," he told her.

"Do you want me to come?"

"No, you finish up in the kitchen. If I need backup, I'll call some of the men."

Edith nodded and returned to the kitchen, thinking that it sounded as if Charles were going off to war. She certainly hoped not. But as she cleaned up, she did pray—very earnestly—that God would keep things under control tonight. Finally, she could stand the suspense no longer. She freshened up, pulled on her coat, scarf, and boots, and trudged on over to the church.

Expecting to see Charles ordering these people, whoever they were, off the church property, she was surprised to see that he was holding one end of a rope with a donkey attached to the other end.

"Come here," he said to her. "Feel this guy's nose."

She walked over and, removing her glove, put her hand on the donkey's warm muzzle. "Very soft." She looked curiously at Charles. "So, what does this mean? Are you letting them stay?"

"I met the owner, George Brown. He owns that little farm just south of here."

"Brown's Eggs?"

"Yes, and other things too. Anyway, he's a really nice guy, and it seems he knows Myrtle—God only knows how that happened. But he's gone to so much trouble first loading and then bringing these animals, and in the snow. Also, Myrtle promised his little girl that she could be an angel tonight. And he's brought bales of straw and pens for the animals ... and, well, I just don't have the heart to turn him away. This is Buster, by the way," he said, nodding to the donkey. "He belongs to April, the little girl." He pointed over to the large side yard next to the church where Myrtle and a little girl were trying to get a sheep into a pen.

"Need any help?" called a voice from behind. And they looked to see Michael and Lauren approaching.

"Welcome to the petting zoo," said Edith.

"She really pulled it off," said Michael as he looked around at the animals in various stages of unloading.

"Well, not actually," said Edith, perhaps a bit too skeptically. "The night isn't over yet. All manner of chaos could still occur."

"Looks like George could use a hand," said Michael, leaving them to go assist George as he urged another sheep out of the truck. Charles followed, leading the donkey as he went.

"Michael told me about visiting George's farm," Lauren said to Edith. "He really enjoyed it. He said George is a really nice guy."

"He's certainly gone to a lot of work," said Edith, trying to get in the spirit of what was feeling more and more like a three-ring circus.

"I think I'll go help Myrtle with the sheep,"

said Lauren, leaving Edith to stand by herself on the sidelines.

"Dear Lord," she prayed quietly. "Please, help this to work out."

"What's going on?" said a woman's voice. Edith turned to see Leslie and Megan approaching now. Illuminated by the truck's brake lights, they trekked through the snow with curious expressions. Edith gave them a brief explanation, and Megan begged to go and pet the animals.

"I'm sure that it's fine," said Edith. "I just wish it weren't so dark out here." Then she remembered Myrtle's lanterns. Of course, that's what they were for. "I'll be right back," she told them.

Back at the inn, she discovered Mr. Benson pouring himself a cup of coffee. "How are you doing this evening?" she asked.

"I'm all right."

"Did you see what's going on across the street?" she asked, glancing nervously up at the mantel clock, worried that Olive could get here any minute, and then things could get messy.

He looked out the window and shook his head. "So, she wasn't making it all up?"

"Making it up?"

"About the live nativity at the church. She had me drive her all over town to put up those flyers, but when I actually saw what they said, I got mad at her. I told her she was nuts."

"Oh, don't worry, you're not the only one who thinks that. I just came over to get the kerosene lanterns. They could use some light over there."

He set down his cup. "That was supposed to be my job."

So, feeling relieved of her duties as well as a bit tired, Edith went up to her room and put her feet up. Oh, she was a little worried about all the details and how Olive was going to react, but as was her usual way, she brought those concerns to the Lord. And then she fell asleep.

When she awoke, it was a little after seven. Oh, dear, she hoped she hadn't missed anything. She threw on her coat and boots and rushed out the door. To her surprise there were cars lined up for as far as she could see, up and down both sides of the street, which meant the small parking lot was probably full too. Feeling as excited as a child, she hurried up to the church to find that the doors were open and people were crowded into the foyer. The church was packed! And the pageant was just starting. Edith just stood there and watched with wonder. Of course, it wasn't perfect. Benjamin Craig, a shepherd, forgot his lines, and little Maggie Turner's angel wings fell off. But how they got those animals to behave during the performance was a mystery to her.

When it was all said and done, the audience clapped and cheered, and Charles stepped forward to announce that the living nativity and refreshments would continue outside. "At least for a while," he told them. "As long as the children and animals can handle the cold. But while they're setting things up, let's all join together for some Christmas carols."

Edith, being in the back of the church, was one of the first ones out when the singing ended. Relieved to be out of the stuffy foyer and in the fresh air, she wasn't prepared for what she saw. It was like a Christmas card. Someone, the men probably, had moved the stable structure outside, and it was flanked by straw bales and illuminated with the kerosene lanterns that Mr. Benson had brought over. Children and animals were in their places, and the effect was amazing. Edith spied Olive and Judy off to one side, quietly coaching the children, but Myrtle didn't seem to be around. Hopefully, they hadn't had fireworks . . . Edith was sure she'd hear all the details later. And, really, Olive should be happy—this was the best Christmas pageant ever, and the turnout was incredible. Not only that, Edith noticed that some people who hadn't even been in the church were already outside, standing on the sidewalk and looking on. It was really something!

15

Edith had a lot to do today. But even as she went about her chores, she felt a general spirit of lightness—a joy that had been missing earlier in the week. She knew that it was because of the pageant last night. It was as if the pageant had put things into perspective.

Unfortunately, it hadn't gone off without a hitch. Later that night Charles had told her that when Olive arrived, she and Myrtle did get into a terrible squabble. "Fortunately, the children were already inside putting on their costumes by then. Judy had gone in to help them, but Olive was absolutely livid that Myrtle had gone behind her back to bring in the livestock. And she didn't care who heard her say so. Of course, our Myrtle didn't do anything to help the situation either. I finally had to step in and tell them both to stop their fighting or leave."

As it turned out, Charles's warning had worked. Edith was just glad that she hadn't had to give it. She wasn't sure that she could've made that kind of an impression on two such strong-willed women.

As usual, Edith had invited a few friends from church, those without family and such, to come to the inn for their annual Christmas Eve party, and she expected up to thirty to attend. Although she'd done a lot of the preparations in advance, there was still much to do, and she spent most of her day in the kitchen. Not that she minded, since her kitchen was her domain, and surprisingly enough, no one was pushing their way into her territory today.

Knowing that some restaurants in town weren't open on Christmas Eve, she had made sure to put a small luncheon buffet out on the dining room table at noon for her guests. And judging by what was left, it appeared they had enjoyed it. All in all, it had been a quiet day at the inn. Peter had invited some of the guests to go sledding on One Tree Hill, and Charles had even gone up there to build a big bonfire. She expected they'd all come home by dusk, if not sooner. They'd be cold and tired and hungry. But she would be ready for them. The party, officially slated to begin at six, could start earlier for the guests at the inn.

Later in the afternoon, she went around the house, putting on Christmas music, turning on the tree lights, lighting candles. She paused where the missing angel once had been, then just sadly shook her head. Perhaps she'd never get to the bottom of it. Maybe little Megan had accidentally broken it, cleaned it up, and hidden the pieces. Her children had been known to do such things without meaning to. Although, if that was the case, for Megan's sake, Edith wished she'd come clean. Guilt like that could stick with a child for years and years to come. *Don't worry about it*, Edith told herself as she turned on the outside lights and looked out at the snow. It was a small thing, really.

Soon the house was bustling with people. It started with those who had been sledding, cold, tired, and hungry, just as she'd expected. But they were in good spirits, and her table full of scrumptious foods hit the spot. Even the Fieldses, who had indulged in sledding too, seemed to have set aside their arguing for a pleasant change. And Michael and Lauren, taken with little Megan, had officially "adopted" her as their new niece. But perhaps most surprising and exciting, at least to Edith, was that Peter and Leslie seemed to have established some sort of bond. She mentioned her suspicions to Charles, and he just winked at her.

Collin and Amy came in at a little before six. Edith hadn't seen them since the night before at the pageant, and then only briefly. She hoped they were doing okay. But they also seemed in good spirits and had even taken some care with their appearance. Collin had on a shirt, slightly wrinkled, with a tie, and Amy had on a long green dress that was very pretty with her eyes.

"How are you feeling?" Edith asked Amy as she led them to the buffet table.

"Okay, I guess. My back hasn't been hurting so much . . ." Then she looked around to see if anyone was listening. "But I'm wondering about these things . . ."

"Things?" Edith looked curiously at Amy.

"Can we go in there?" Amy nodded to the

kitchen, and Edith led her through the swinging doors.

"What is it?" asked Edith, concerned.

"I don't think I'm having contractions," Amy explained, "because it doesn't hurt, and aren't contractions supposed to hurt?"

Edith nodded, then reconsidered. "Well, not always so much at first. First it just gets tight around your abdomen, like the muscles are clenching."

"Yes, it feels kind of like that."

"But, of course, there are Braxton Hicks too. They feel like that. Goodness, I had Braxton Hicks for weeks before Katie was born. It almost made me crazy."

"Maybe that's what this is," said Amy hopefully. "I really don't want to have this baby until we're in California."

Edith patted her on the shoulder. "And you probably won't. I've heard that it's unusual for first babies to come early. Mine was two weeks late."

"Oh, good."

So they went back out and joined the others. Mr. Benson had come down now, wearing a white shirt and red bow tie. "You look very festive," Edith told him as she handed him a plate for the buffet table.

"And so does this!" he said as he began to fill it.

Soon other friends began to arrive, and it wasn't long until the house was filled with people and laughter and visiting. Almost the same as when her children were home, Edith thought as she went to the kitchen to refill a cheese tray. But not quite. Still, it was certainly better than being alone, and she thought that her guests would probably agree with her. But as she considered this, it occurred to her that she hadn't seen much of Myrtle. Of course, Myrtle, with her quirky ways, could be waiting for just the right moment before she came out and made some kind of entrance, perhaps even with a speech about the true meaning of Christmas. No need to hurry that up. Edith took the tray out and discovered that the cheese puffs needed replenishing.

Peter, a good piano player, had made himself comfortable playing Christmas carols in the living room with a jolly little circle gathered around him doing their best to sing, although only a few seemed to know all the words. Others had broken into various groups and were visiting comfortably, and as far as Edith could see, everyone was engaged and having a pretty good time. But for the second time tonight, she didn't see Myrtle anywhere. Finally, she decided to ask if Charles had seen her. It was entirely possible that Myrtle had come down while Edith was busy in the kitchen and gotten into some kind of a fracas with someone, perhaps even Mr. Benson, although he seemed to be enjoying himself as he looked at Millie Mortenson's pictures of grandchildren.

"I haven't seen her," Charles told Edith after she inquired.

"Not at all?"

"No. Come to think of it, I haven't seen her since last night."

"Not even at breakfast?" asked Edith. "I was so busy in the kitchen that I didn't really pay close attention to who came and went."

"I was only there for about thirty minutes, but Myrtle didn't come down during that time. That's probably why I had such a pleasant breakfast." He smiled a bit sheepishly. "Sorry, that wasn't very gracious of me. But, if you think about it, things are going rather well this evening. Why push Myrtle into being social if she'd rather keep to herself?"

She considered this. "Yes, she may be using this time to think about things. But I do hope that she's not feeling badly about last night. Do you think that's the problem?"

He patted her on the back. "My guess is that she's simply worn out from all the activities yesterday. She probably grabbed a quick breakfast when neither of us were looking . . . and don't forget that you left all those luncheon goodies out, which I'm sure she helped herself to . . . and perhaps after that she took a little afternoon nap. Don't worry. I'm sure she'll be down here before you know it."

"You're probably right."

After that, Edith had her hands full just keeping the food coming as well as taking time to visit with her guests, so much so that she hardly noticed that nearly two hours had passed and Myrtle still hadn't come down.

"Has anyone seen Myrtle today?" she finally asked a few guests. But no one seemed to have seen her.

"I haven't seen her since yesterday." Mr. Benson chuckled. "Not that I mind so much."

"She's probably tired out from yesterday," Edith told him, echoing Charles's earlier explanation, although she wasn't so sure anymore.

Finally, it was getting late, the party was

dwindling to an end, and Myrtle still hadn't made an appearance. Charles still felt certain that the old woman was simply catching up on her rest. "She had a very busy few days," he reminded Edith. "And she's not exactly a young woman. Besides, tomorrow's Christmas, and I'm sure she'll be up bright and early to interrupt your quiet morning time. Just wait and see."

Edith thought he was right, but she still felt a bit concerned when she went to bed. What if something *was* wrong? Perhaps she should've checked on the old woman earlier just to be sure, but now it was so late that she didn't like the idea of disturbing her. Edith had done that with an elderly guest once before, waking the poor old fellow out of a perfectly good sleep, only to get scolded for her intrusion. And she certainly didn't wish to be reproached by Myrtle of all people. Charles was probably right. She'd see Myrtle soon enough in the morning.

16

Christmas morning came, and Edith got all the way through her devotional reading without being interrupted. She fixed a festive Christmas breakfast, with Charles's help, and still no Myrtle. Even the other guests noticed the old woman's absence. And finally Edith couldn't stand it any longer. Goodness, what if Myrtle had died in her sleep?

"I'm going to go check on her," she announced, then glancing at Charles, she considered asking him to join her. But that might alarm the other guests. And this was, after

all, Christmas. Edith was probably just blowing this thing all out of proportion.

"I'll come with you," said Charles, standing. Edith wanted to hug him and say thanks,
but she simply nodded.

"I'm sure she's fine," Charles said as they
went up the stairs. "But I do understand your
concern."

"She's normally such an early riser," said
Edith weakly, trying not to fear the worst.

Now they were standing in front of the
door to the Green Meadow Room, the room
where Myrtle was staying. Edith tapped on
the door, first lightly, then louder. But there
was no response. "Myrtle?" she called, waiting. Nothing but silence.

"It's probably locked," said Edith, reaching
into her pocket for the master key. But before
she got it out, Charles had already tried the
door, and it opened. Edith took in a quick
breath, bracing herself for whatever might be
in there, but when the door swung open they
could see the neatly made bed, and as they
went inside, everything seemed in perfect
order. Almost as if Myrtle had never been
there at all. And she certainly wasn't there
now. Everything was just as tidy as it had

been after Edith straightened and replaced linens yesterday.

"Where is she?" said Edith, feeling a bit lost.

"Where are her things?" asked Charles as he continued looking around the orderly room as if he expected to find a clue.

Edith didn't know what to think. "I have no idea."

"Look," said Charles, pointing at something on the bureau.

Edith came over to see that it was her porcelain angel. "My angel!" she exclaimed. "What is it—"

"There's something underneath it," said Charles as he carefully lifted the angel and picked up the small white envelope with the picture of a shepherd and lamb on one side, stationery provided by their inn.

"To the innkeepers." Edith read the front of the envelope as Charles handed it to her. She slowly opened it, and the first thing she noticed was the money inside. "What is this?" She handed the bills to Charles, then proceeded to read the juvenile-looking handwriting out loud.

"Thanks for your hospitality. You got a nice

place here. Sorry I couldn't stick around to say good-bye, but it's time for me to go. Collin and Amy can use my room now that I'm gone. I have one more week paid up, and the money enclosed is for any extra days or in case they need gas money. I know you'll take care of it for me. Sincerely, Myrtle."

"So she's really gone." Edith looked around the room one more time, almost in disbelief. "I was prepared to have her around for another week."

Charles just shook his head. "But how did she leave? She had no car. Did you see anyone coming to pick her up yesterday?"

"No . . ."

"Do you think someone might've picked her up on Friday night, during the Christmas pageant? There were so many people there, it's possible that she arranged to be quietly picked up and we just didn't notice."

"I suppose . . ." Still, Edith thought it was odd. "But I don't know why she would be so secretive. Myrtle wasn't exactly a private person, you know. She didn't really seem to care what people thought of her. Why would she leave so quietly?"

"I don't know." Charles frowned. "I hope I didn't offend her when I told her and Olive to stop arguing. But I didn't single her out. I addressed Olive in the same manner."

"Oh, I don't think Myrtle was easily offended," said Edith, even though she'd had a similar concern earlier. She just didn't want Charles to feel guilty.

"You don't think she would've tried to make it out of here on foot, do you?" said Charles uncertainly.

"Oh, I don't think so . . ."

"Just the same, maybe I should drive around a bit, check around town, just in case. I'd feel horrible to think that old woman is out on the road, in the snow, and on Christmas."

"Yes, that's a good idea. I know I'd appreciate it. But before you leave, let me go take a look at her registration form. Maybe I can give her home a call and see if she's arrived safely."

"Yes. That's a good plan."

They hurried downstairs, and Edith searched in her file until she found Myrtle's registration form. But other than her name, the form was blank. "I thought you said she filled this out," she said to Charles.

He adjusted his glasses to look at it. "Well, I thought she did." He scratched his head now. "But then I remember she wanted to pay in cash, and so I was more focused on doing the math and making her change, and I suppose I just dropped the form into your file and never really looked at it."

"This is very weird, Charles. Someone drops this eccentric woman off, she pays for two weeks' lodging in cash, and then she disappears after one week. It could almost make someone think that she's some deranged patient who escaped from some institution."

"Or an angel."

She turned and looked at Charles. "You don't really think?"

He kind of laughed. "Well, certainly an odd angel."

"Very odd."

"Edith?"

She turned to see Collin, and his face looked frightened. "What is it?" she asked.

"Amy!" he exclaimed. "She's in labor. What should I do?"

By now several of the guests had gathered around, witnessing this little spectacle.

"Oh!" Edith looked at Charles. "Should we drive them to the hospital?"

"No," said Collin. "Amy refuses to go to the

hospital. I already asked her, and she got really mad at me. I promised her that she wouldn't have to go, but now I'm not so sure. What should I do?"

"Can you get her into the house?" asked Edith. "Can she make it up the stairs?"

"Up the stairs?" Collin looked confused now.

"Myrtle left. She wanted you kids to have her room."

Collin brightened a bit. "Really?"

"Yeah, but can Amy get in here okay?"

"I'll go see."

"I'll come help," said Charles.

Then Edith got on the phone. She hated to disturb Helen on Christmas Day, but Helen had made her promise. And as it turned out, Helen sounded quite pleased. "No, it's not a problem, Edith. We're not really doing anything at all. It's just Clarence and me. I'll have him drive me right over, well, as soon as I get some things together first."

It was quite amazing how the other guests stepped in to help. Leslie, the person who had most recently given birth, took it on herself to help coach Amy through labor. Meanwhile Lauren and Michael entertained little

Megan with games and books. Edith, distracted in trying to help Helen and Leslie and making sure they had what they needed for Amy, was forced to let her regular chores go, but Carmen and Jim Fields jumped right in, actually putting away all the breakfast things and cleaning the kitchen. And Mr. Benson and Helen's husband, Clarence, enjoyed several games of chess.

During this hectic time at the bed and breakfast, Charles was out scouring the town of Christmas Valley. He even called Peter and asked him to look around a bit too. But finally the two of them met on a deserted Main Street and, certain that Myrtle wasn't out shivering in an alley somewhere, decided to return to the inn.

Amy's labor intensified in the afternoon, and everyone continued to pitch in to help, taking turns running things upstairs and helping to get Christmas dinner ready in the kitchen. All the guests offered to straighten their own rooms and replenish their own linens. Edith was actually able to sit down and put her feet up for a few minutes.

Angela Myrtle was born at 3:45 p.m. After helping Helen to clean off the squirming wet infant and wrapping her into a snug flannel blanket, Edith went down to fetch her kitchen scales. Little Angela weighed in at seven pounds and four ounces.

"Angela *Myrtle*?" Edith queried as she adjusted the pillow beneath the tired mother's head.

Amy smiled. "Angela is for Collin's grandmother. Myrtle is for the kind woman who allowed us to stay in this amazing room." She looked around the room, with its soothing green colors and peaceful pastoral pictures adorning the walls, and smiled. "I feel like I'm in heaven right now. I never dreamed I'd have my baby in such a beautiful place."

"Myrtle's timing couldn't have been better," said Edith as she gathered up some linens.

"Where did she go, anyway?" asked Collin. He was sitting at the end of Amy's bed now, cradling his brand-new daughter in his arms.

"We don't really know," admitted Edith. "But it seemed her mission here was done."

"Mission?"

Edith smiled. "I think God gives us all some kind of mission."

*   *   *

Somehow the turkey and dressing and all the rest of the Christmas dinner made its way to the big dining room table on time. And as Charles and Edith and all their house-guests, minus the new little family upstairs and plus Helen and Clarence and Peter, gathered together, Charles invited them to all bow their heads in a Christmas blessing. Before Charles said "amen," he specifically thanked God for sending them Myrtle.

"So, do you really believe that God sent Myrtle?" queried Mr. Benson with a some-what skeptical expression across his brow.

Charles nodded solemnly. "Yes, I do. I'm just sorry that I didn't notice sooner."

That's when everyone at the table began to share their own personal experiences and exchanges with the peculiar woman. And most had to agree that Myrtle had indeed rubbed them wrongly, at least to begin with, but at the same time she had touched them at some level—some deep level where they all needed a touch.

Certainly, not everyone was convinced that Myrtle had literally been sent by God via a direct route from heaven. But some weren't so sure she hadn't.

"Perhaps it's not so important that we know where Myrtle came from for certain," Charles finally said. "As long as we believe that God can use someone as unexpected and unconventional as Myrtle to touch our lives. Maybe that's what really matters."

But Edith felt certain that Myrtle was indeed an angel. Only, like her husband, she wished that she'd come to this realization sooner. She also wished that she'd treated Myrtle with a bit more love and respect. Although that might've spoiled things for the strange old woman, blowing her cover, so to speak—because, Edith suspected, Myrtle's mission may not have been accomplished if she hadn't performed it incognito.

Melody Carlson is the prolific author of more than a hundred books, including fiction, nonfiction, and gift books for adults, young adults, and children. She is also the author of *Three Days* and *The Gift of Christmas Present*. Her writing has won several awards, including a Gold Medallion for *King of the Stable* (Crossway, 1998) and a Romance Writers of America Rita Award for *Homeward* (Multnomah, 1997). She lives with her husband in Sisters, Oregon.